"Do you think we could do this again sometime?"

"Hmm…I'll have to think that one over a bit," Jackson said, pretending to contemplate her question. "Getting you back behind the wheel would mean I would no longer be needed to take you and Lucas here and there. I'm not so sure I'm ready to give that up."

"I would think you would be relieved," she told him with a smile.

"You'd be wrong."

Her smile softened with his admission. "I'm realistic if anything. I know I have a long way to go before I'm going to be comfortable behind the wheel, but I want my independence back. Want to be the kind of mother Lucas deserves."

His expression softened even more. "Your son is already blessed to have you for his mother, whether you drive or not. He's just too young to really appreciate what he has, but that will come. Right now, he's still working through a lot of pain and grief."

Reaching over, she covered his hand with hers, giving it a squeeze. "I've missed you, Jackson Wade."

Kat Brookes is an award-winning author and past Romance Writers of America Golden Heart® Award finalist. She is married to her childhood sweetheart and has been blessed with two beautiful daughters. She loves writing stories that can both make you smile and touch your heart. Kat is represented by Michelle Grajkowski with 3 Seas Literary Agency. Read more about Kat and her upcoming releases at katbrookes.com. Email her at katbrookes@comcast.net. Facebook: Kat Brookes.

Books by Kat Brookes

Love Inspired

Bent Creek Blessings

The Cowboy's Little Girl
The Rancher's Baby Surprise
Hometown Christmas Gift

Texas Sweethearts

Her Texas Hero
His Holiday Matchmaker
Their Second Chance Love

Hometown Christmas Gift

Kat Brookes

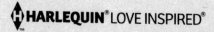

Recycling programs
for this product may
not exist in your area.

LOVE INSPIRED BOOKS

ISBN-13: 978-1-335-47954-9

Hometown Christmas Gift

www.Harlequin.com

Printed in U.S.A.

But let him ask in faith, nothing wavering.
For he that wavereth is like a wave of the sea
driven with the wind and tossed.

—*James* 1:6

This book is dedicated to my cousin Kathy Dillan and to my good friend Melissa Huddleston. Two women very near and dear to my heart. I'm so grateful to have you both in my life.

Chapter One

Lainie Michaels lifted the snow-dusted doormat again, thinking she might have missed the house key her brother was supposed to have left there for her. Nothing. She tried the door again, but it was locked up good and tight. Straightening, she blew on her chilled fingers to warm them and then slipped her gloves back on. At least she'd had the forethought to purchase winter coats for her and her son before moving back to Wyoming.

"I don't want to be here!" Lainie's seven-year-old son, Lucas, bellowed behind her, stomping his tiny foot in defiance.

Lainie turned from the locked front door and forced a smile as she prepared to face yet another one of her son's emotional thunderstorms. "Honey, you'll like living here in Bent Creek." At least, she prayed he would. More than anything, she wanted her son to be the sweet, loving little boy he used to be before she'd taken his joy away.

"It's cold here. I wanna go home," he replied, his tiny brows furrowed into a deep-set scowl.

Early December in Bent Creek could be cold. Especially when her son was accustomed to California winters, but it was a little soon for any real snow accumulation. Lainie's gaze moved past Lucas to the large, white flakes coming down from the wintry sky above. Then again, maybe it wasn't. Cold or not, while living in California, she'd missed the beauty Wyoming winters could bring, the sight of the distant mountains and vast land surrounding her brother's place, the home she had grown up in, glistening with newly fallen snow. Especially during the holidays.

Looking down at her son, Lainie suddenly felt overwhelmed by emotion and exhausted from having gotten up before dawn that morning to catch their flight. And then, after a three-hour layover in Denver before finally landing in Rock Springs, Wyoming, the nearest airport to Bent Creek, they'd had to take a taxi to her brother's place a good fifty-minutes away.

"We are home," she told Lucas. Or, at least what would be their home until they found a place of their own in Bent Creek. Even if she changed her mind about staying there permanently, which she hadn't, they would have no way to leave. The taxi that brought them there had already driven off. They'd sold their two-bedroom condo in downtown Sacramento, sent a few boxes of their personal items ahead to her brother, Justin, a week prior to flying home and then placed the remainder of their things in storage until they found a home of their own and could have them brought out.

"This isn't my home," her son said, his voice cracking with anger.

"It is now, sweetie," Lainie said softly, praying that she'd made the right decision in coming there.

"You take everything away!" her son sobbed, tears of frustration and anger now filling his hazel eyes. "Even my dad. I hate you!" Turning, he sprinted off the porch and disappeared around the side of the house.

Lainie ran over to the railing and leaned out, watching as Lucas ran away from the house, no doubt to the fort his uncle had built for him two summers before. "Lucas!" she called after him, hot tears blurring her vision. It wasn't the first time he had run off, and it wasn't the first time her baby boy's words had left her feeling broken. Her son hated her, and she couldn't even blame him for it. He'd lost his father, and it was all her fault. A lump formed in Lainie's throat as the memory of that night surfaced, making it hard to swallow. No amount of "I'm sorrys" could ever make up for the pain she had caused her little boy. She'd never forget the look of confusion on his face when she'd told him his father was gone, and then fear and bone-deep sorrow that slowly settled in as her son processed her words. It had nearly broken her. A mother's words were supposed to wrap their child in love and make them feel safe, not shatter their entire world.

The sudden sound of hoofbeats had Lainie turning, a small gasp leaving her lips as she took in the sight of a man seated astride a beautiful buckskin gelding. He came to a stop just on the other side of the porch at the far end of Justin's house. Although he wore his cowboy hat low and the collar of his leather duster lifted to block the icy, whirling flakes, she'd recognize those dark green eyes of his anywhere.

"Lainie," Jackson Wade greeted her, his voice so much deeper than it had been when he'd spent time at her house when they were growing up. Jackson had always been her brother's best friend and also her heart's greatest weakness.

Her stomach felt as though she'd just taken a steep drop on a roller-coaster ride. The last time she'd seen Jackson had been in the hospital in Las Vegas after he'd been injured while bull riding at Nationals. Only Jackson hadn't known she'd been there, because she'd not been able to step beyond the open door. Just seeing him lying there, eyes closed, machines surrounding him, had been more than she could take. Especially since she blamed herself for his being there. Had lived with the self-imposed guilt of it for years. Oh, why did their paths have to cross at that very moment?

Lainie turned away, looking off into the direction her son had run, trying desperately to collect herself. "Justin's not home," she said as she hurried to swipe a poorly timed tear from her cheek with her gloved hand. Jackson Wade was the last person she wanted to see her in such an emotionally vulnerable state. In fact, she'd prefer not to cross paths with him altogether, now or ever. Unfortunately, "ever" wasn't in the realm of possibility, considering they were both going to be living in the same small town.

"I know," he replied as the sound of booted footsteps treading up the porch steps came from a few feet behind her.

She cast a fretful glance back over her shoulder as he strode toward her, her attention drawn to his slightly off-kilter gait. *A limp she had caused*, she thought to herself, guilt making her turn away once more. She couldn't bear to see the man who had broken her heart. The man she had in turn broken physically.

A gentle hand came to rest on her shoulder. "Lainie," he said, his voice filled with concern.

Jackson, she thought in silent response. Her first love. An unrequited love. But one her heart had never quite gotten over. Even after she had married Will Michaels, a kind, supportive man, the handsome cowboy standing behind her had still maintained a special place in her heart. One of the reasons she had done her best to come home to visit only when she knew Jackson would be away, running stock to the various rodeos. And then after her husband's death not quite two years before, she had avoided Bent Creek altogether. For her son, who was not dealing well with his grief. She thought that she needed to keep his routine as unchanged and normal as possible. And, if she were being completely honest with herself, it was also because of the feelings she still harbored for Jackson. Feelings she should have been able to put to rest after she'd gotten together with Will, but her stubborn heart had refused to cooperate. Staying away from Bent Creek, away from Jackson, had been the only way she could think of to assuage the guilt she felt.

"Are you okay?"

No, she wasn't. But it was no less than she deserved. She nodded. "I'm fine." How much of her conversation, of her son's resentful words, had Jackson overheard? She couldn't bear the thought of anyone thinking badly of Lucas. "Just a little family disagreement."

His large hand fell away, and she found herself wishing it back, needing the comfort that small gesture had provided her. "I'd be happy to have a talk with him if you think that would help matters," he offered.

Lainie forced herself to turn and face him, but kept

her gaze fixed on the front of Jackson's shirt instead of on the pity she knew she would see in those eyes. When had his shoulders grown so incredibly wide? "Thank you," she managed, "but no. I need to see to this on my own." Just as she had been since her husband's passing.

"Then can I at least help you go look for your son?"

"No," she said a little more adamantly, shaking her head. She didn't want Jackson's help. It had been hard enough turning to her brother as it was. She was Lucas's mother. *She* should have been the one to make things right again for her son. "I know where he'll be."

"In the fort?" he replied.

Of course Jackson would know about the small, wooden fort her brother had built for Lucas in the woods behind his house, just beyond the edge of the yard. He and Justin knew pretty much everything about each other. But then they were close. Had been since Justin's first day of school in Bent Creek, after their parents had adopted him and Lainie and brought them to the small, welcoming town to live.

"Yes," she said with a sigh. The counselor she had taken her son to not quite six months before had told Lainie that there would be times when Lucas would need time and space to grieve and sort through his feelings. She'd given him that, but it hadn't seemed to make a difference. Her son's resentment toward her was always simmering close to the surface.

"Is there anything I can do to help?"

"Only if you're a locksmith," Lainie muttered.

He chuckled, his chin lifting just enough to free his face from the cocoon his collar had formed around it. The warm sound of it drew her gaze upward until it came to rest on his face, one that had grown even more handsome with age. His chestnut hair was close-cropped under his well-worn cowboy hat, and he wore just a hint of sideburns alongside his clean-shaven face. "It just so happens I can help you out," he replied with that lone-dimpled grin she had never forgotten as he held up a small brass house key. "Justin called to tell me that he'd forgotten to leave a key under the doormat for guests he had coming to stay with him and asked if I could run the spare he'd given me over to the house."

Guests? Had her brother avoided telling Jackson that she was the guest he was referring to? Was he unsure his friend would be comfortable with the given task if he knew the whole truth?

"Long-term guests," Lainie supplied with a troubled frown. "Lucas and I are going to be living with my brother until we can find a place of our own."

His eyes widened in surprise. "You're moving home?"

"Moved," she corrected. "As of today."

He nodded as if struggling to find a response to the clearly unexpected news. Lainie found herself wondering if the kiss they'd shared all those years ago still lingered in the back of his thoughts as it did in hers. And not in the way a first kiss shared between two people should.

"It's been hard on Lucas dealing with life in Sacramento since his father's passing," she tried to explain without going into detail.

"I can imagine it would be," Jackson said. Then his expression grew serious. "I never got to tell you how sorry I was to hear about your loss."

"You sent us a card and those beautiful wind chimes," she said with a grateful smile.

A frown pulled at his mouth now. "I really am sorry. I should have done more."

She shook her head. "You thought about us and that meant a lot." She reached for the key he was still holding in his hand, feeling the chill of the metal through the fingertips of her glove. "Thank you for going to the trouble of running this over to us in this weather." She glanced past him. "And by horse, at that."

"I can still ride," he muttered. "Just not competitively."

The guilt that filled her at his reminder was almost painful. He'd loved the rodeo and she had taken that from him. "I just meant that you could have driven the key over," she hurried to explain. "It's cold out."

He shrugged, his broad shoulders lifting and dropping beneath his leather coat. "Cold's never bothered me. And it wasn't any trouble running this over to you. And, Lainie…" he said, their gazes meeting.

"Yes," she replied, unable to look away, and her heart skittered, just as it used to do when she was a lovesick teenager. That thought brought Lainie immediately back to reality. She was not that same girl. She was a widowed mother of a very lost child, and Jackson was no longer that same boy she had once known. He was a grown man with responsibilities, part of which revolved around the very thing that had kept them apart—the rodeo.

He smiled down at her. "Welcome home."

"Thank you." She glanced in the direction Lucas had run off in. "I should go see to my son." She just prayed he'd had time to calm down enough for them to be able to talk. She hated watching her precious little boy slip so far away from her emotionally. Hopefully, her brother would be able to help bring him back.

"If I can ever do anything…" He let the offer trail off.

"We'll be fine," she replied. "But thank you for offering."

Jackson tipped his hat and then turned to leave.

Lainie watched him go, tears filling her eyes as she took in the change in the confident gait she remembered. That slight hitch to his step made her heart ache. Jackson could have died that day, and she would have had to live with that guilt for the rest of her life, just as she did with her husband's death.

You take away everything! Even my dad. I hate you! Jackson flinched at the memory of those harshly spoken words. Words that had to have broken Lainie's heart. Will had died in a car accident. Why would her son blame Lainie for that?

Lainie, he thought to himself as he parked his truck in front of the sheriff's office, regret filling him. The girl he had cared so much about. The girl whose heart he'd broken. If he had the chance to do it all over again, would he have gone about things differently? He'd asked himself that question more times than he could count over the years, but he remained torn over the answer. Lainie had been his best friend's little sister, which had made him keep his growing feelings for her to himself. It had seemed like a line he shouldn't cross. But he had and kissing her at the town's annual Old West Festival Dance that night had been both eye-opening and life changing.

Jackson stepped down from his truck, closed the

door and headed for the nearby building. He let himself inside and made his way to Justin's office. Shoving open the door, he stepped inside. "You might have told me," he said, his words tight.

His friend, the town's sheriff, glanced up from paperwork and then sat back in his chair. "Would you have gone over to my place if I had?" he asked matter-of-factly.

It bothered him that his friend had a point. If he had known that Lainie and her son were the "guests" Justin had been referring to when he'd called to ask his favor, he might very well have sent someone in his place to deliver the key. He hadn't been prepared to see Lainie again. Had even prepared himself emotionally to never see her again. Truth was, he'd made his choice a long time ago and understood her reasons for making certain their paths never crossed. All he could do was respect her wishes. A part of him was grateful for her determined avoidance of him. It meant she hadn't had to see him as he was now, after the accident, hobbling about instead of moving with the sure-footed grace he'd once had.

"Your silence speaks volumes," Justin said, pushing away from his desk to stand. "But you need to get past whatever it was that happened between the two of you before Lainie went off to college, because Lainie's going to be living here. You will be seeing her, like it or not."

If only it were that simple. "Nothing happened," Jackson replied with a frown. Only because he'd stopped it from going anywhere. When Lainie had kissed him that night after they'd stepped outside for some fresh air following a round of heel-kicking dances and then a long, slow dance, he'd been taken by surprise. He should have put an end to things right then and there, but he hadn't. He'd kissed her back. And when the kiss ended, all the emotions she'd held back for so long spilled out of her. She loved him. Wanted to give up the full-ride academic scholarship she gotten to go to San Diego State University and stay in Bent Creek instead, so she could be with him. Lainie would have traded an opportunity very few were ever blessed with to be *his* girl. And someday, he knew, she would have resented him for it.

"All I know is that Lainie thought the world revolved around you. To the point I thought that maybe someday…" Justin shook his head. "And then she began dating Will, marrying him right out of college."

It was when she'd called him with news of her engagement that he'd been taken down emotionally, causing him to lose focus that night during his last ride in the rodeo finals in Vegas, giving Lucky Shamrock the upper hand. The sixteen-hundred-pound bull had put an end to Jackson's career with one good stomp on Jackson's leg. In that one day, he lost the girl he'd loved enough to let go, and then his career as a professional bull rider.

"It doesn't matter now," Jackson told him. "The past is in the past."

"That means you and Lainie should be able to mend whatever fences the two of you have that need mending."

This time Jackson didn't try to deny what his friend had called him out on. He was just grateful he hadn't pressed for details. That kiss he'd shared with Lainie all those years ago had meant something to Jackson.

More than it should have. "You still should have told me she was coming," he said with a troubled frown.

Justin settled a hip atop the corner of his desk and folded his arms. "So you could leave town?"

"Why would I do that?" he asked.

"You and I both know that you would have done everything in your power to avoid her, all because of that barely noticeable limp you have, and right now Lainie needs you."

Barely noticeable? Did his friend truly not realize how his injury had affected him, not only physically but mentally? And Lainie had been the one doing the avoiding. He was so busy mentally defending himself that it took a moment for Justin's last statement to sink in. *Lainie needs you.*

Jackson met his friend's sober gaze. "What are you talking about?"

Justin stood and crossed the room to close his office door. Then he turned to face him. "What I'm about to tell you doesn't leave this room. My sister will have my head if Mom and Dad get wind of this. Lainie's hoping things will change and they'll never need to know what's been going on."

He'd never seen his friend so serious. "It stays here," Jackson promised with a nod.

Justin returned to his desk, sinking into the chair with a heavy sigh. "Lainie is moving home because she's emotionally wrung out and needed to get away from Sacramento."

"Understandable," he replied, his heart going out to Lainie. "She was widowed at twenty-eight, left to raise a young son all on her own."

"She wouldn't have had to handle anything on her

own if only she had come home after Will died," Justin said, a hint of frustration lacing his words.

"Maybe Lainie needed to at least try to handle things on her own," Jackson pointed out. "Know that she could stand on her own two feet. Whatever her reason may be, it's safe to say the past couple of years, twenty months to be exact, couldn't have been easy for her. Or for Lucas, for that matter," he added, recalling the boy's angry outburst.

"You know the exact number of months?"

"It happened to Lainie," Jackson replied.

Justin nodded. "Sort of burns itself into one's memory, doesn't it? And you're right. It hasn't been easy for her. Granted, Lainie always tried to sound strong whenever we talked on the phone, but I could hear the strain of what she's been through in her voice, having to cope with such a tragedy on her own. I know when we went out there for Will's funeral Lucas was angry with God for taking his father. We all talked to him, trying to get him to see that his anger shouldn't be directed at the Lord, but at the bad choices people sometimes make. Like the teenager who ran that red light that night, causing the accident. Lainie said Lucas had been coming around, but then eight months ago he suddenly began acting out again. Not only at home, but at school and church as well."

"Sounds like his grief is finally surfacing," Jackson said, his heart going out to the little boy, who'd lost his father so young, and to Lainie, whose husband had been taken from her so tragically.

"It needs to," his friend said. "Grief tends to fester when it's shoved aside. Look at how it affected Garrett."

Not only had Jackson and his brothers lost a sister, but his older brother had also lost his high school sweetheart. It had taken Hannah, Garrett's new wife, and her son, Austin, to bring joy fully back into his life.

"I don't want to even think about Lucas holding in his grief for seventeen years like my brother did," Jackson said with a frown.

"Lainie hopes their moving back to Bent Creek, where Lucas will also have his grandparents and myself to turn to when things are troubling him, might be what my nephew needs to pull him from this grief-driven anger he's been experiencing."

Jackson could tell there were issues going on between Lainie and her son but didn't know to what extent. "From what I witnessed today, when I took the key over to your sister, Lainie isn't overreacting where her son is concerned."

Justin's brows furrowed. "Why? What did you see?"

"It was more what I overheard. Their voices were raised, at least her son's was, when I rode up to your porch," Jackson explained. "Lucas was having a meltdown of sorts and then ran off. Lainie doesn't know I overheard their exchange of words, and I'd appreciate it if things could stay that way. Sounds like she's got enough on her plate already without adding embarrassment to all the other emotions she's dealing with right now."

"I appreciate that," his friend said, concern creasing his brow. "I had intended to take the day off and be home waiting for them when they came, but they arrived a couple days ahead of schedule and I am tied up here at work for several more hours."

An impatient tapping sounded at the office door.

"Excuse me," Justin said apologetically as he stood and crossed the room to answer it.

"Sheriff," Mrs. Baxter, the middle-aged reception- ist who worked the front desk, said a bit breathlessly, a troubled frown marring her features. "I'm sorry to interrupt, but Kathy Culler just called. Todd—that is Deputy Culler—has had an accident."

"How bad?" Justin pressed, his words pulling Jack- son back to the present.

"Bad," she said fretfully. "Apparently, Deputy Culler fell off his ladder while putting Christmas lights up on their roof and broke his hip. Kathy told me they'd just taken him back for emergency surgery."

Justin dragged a hand back through his dark brown hair. "The break must have been a serious one."

She nodded. "Kathy isn't one to get too overwrought about things, but she was definitely in a panicked state when she called to let us know."

Jackson said a silent prayer for the injured man, knowing firsthand how hard recovery could be for a badly broken hip. Especially for an older man. Deputy Culler was in his late fifties and had been employed by Bent Creek's Sheriff's Department for as long as Jack- son could remember. Could probably even have been sheriff somewhere along the way if he hadn't had such an aversion to all the extra paperwork and responsibil- ity the position demanded, stressors of the job Justin handled with ease.

"I'll head over to the hospital to sit with her for a while as soon as I finish up here," Justin told his fraz- zled secretary. "In the meantime, call Deputy Mitch- ell and explain the situation. See if there's any chance he could cut his vacation short to come back and take over Deputy Culler's shift. Tell him we'll make it up to him."

"I doubt he'll be able to," she replied, her frown deepening. "He's on a ship somewhere in Alaska."

Justin sighed. "I forgot he was going to be seeing Alaska by cruise ship."

She managed a slight smile. "Probably because his vacations usually include a remote cabin somewhere. Not a fancy hotel on the water. Besides, you've got a lot on your mind with your sister and her son coming home to live with you."

Jackson's brows knitted together. Justin had told his receptionist about Lainie moving home, but had chosen to keep the news from him? Sure, Jackson had mentioned knowing there were issues between him and Lainie. But it made Jackson wonder exactly what his friend did know. Had Lainie opened up to her brother about the heartbreak Jackson had caused her? About how he had crushed all of her girlhood dreams about true love?

"I could probably reach him through the cruise line's main office," Mrs. Baxter suggested. "He could probably catch a flight home from his next stop."

"No," Justin said, shaking his head with a sigh. "Deputy Vance and I can split Deputy Culler's shifts between us."

"Only two of you doing everything?" she said, growing wide-eyed beneath the rim of her rhinestone-lined cat's-eye glasses.

"It'll only be for ten or so days," he assured her. "Then Deputy Mitchell will be back and can take over his share of the extra workload. In the meantime, I'll see if we can bring in additional help until we're back to a full crew."

She shrugged. "I suppose that's all we can do for now. Thank the Lord above that Bent Creek is a peace-loving town or we would be in real trouble."

Justin offered her a reassuring smile. "If that was an issue, I'd just deputize Jackson here to fill in. He's good with a rope. Could lasso any criminal who dared to step foot in our little town."

The older woman looked his way and Jackson smiled. "If it ever came down to it, I wouldn't even wait for him to ask. I'd volunteer." His gaze slid over to Justin. "Because that's what friends are for. To help each other out in times of need." And Justin had been there for him plenty of times over the years. Especially after Lucky Shamrock had sent Jackson to the hospital with a crushed leg and fractured hip. Justin was always checking in on him. He'd driven Jackson to countless physical therapy sessions and had picked Jackson up those times depression threatened to claim him.

"That's good to know," the older woman said, sounding a little less harried. Looking to Justin, she said, "I'll call Kathy and let her know you'll be stop-ping by."

"Thank you," Justin said, closing the door behind the older woman's departing form. Then he turned to Jackson. "This couldn't have happened at a worse time."

"Not so sure Todd had much say-so over the tim-ing," Jackson pointed out with a small grin, hoping to ease some of his friend's stress.

"Maybe not, but the fact remains I'm going to be spending most of my time working."

"In other words, nothing's changed," he pointed out. His friend was very committed to the position he'd been appointed to and worked long hours already as it was.

"I had hoped to take a little time off to spend time with Lainie and Lucas, but that won't be possible now," Justin said with a heavy sigh.

"I'm sure she'll understand."

"Maybe so. But Lainie was counting on me to do things with Lucas his father might have done if he were still here. With Todd out of commission, and Deputy Mitchell away on a lengthy vacation, I'm going to have far less time to spend with my nephew. Intentional or not, I'm letting my sister down when she needs me the most."

"Maybe your dad can fill in until your schedule frees up a little," Jackson suggested.

Justin looked to him. "Dad? You do recall that he's seventy years old now, with arthritis in both knees."

Jackson nodded. Justin and Lainie's parents had been in their early- to midforties when they'd adopted the orphaned siblings. His friend had been five at the time and Lainie only two, and they had been loved beyond measure by their adoptive parents—the only parents they had ever really known. "I suppose that would make it difficult to play football with Lucas, or to go on hikes with him through the woods." And all the things they used to do with their fathers as boys.

"Jackson," Justin said, meeting his gaze. "You've always been like a brother to me. To Lainie as well."

Not always, Jackson thought, recalling the kiss. Guilt nudged at him. "I feel the same way."

"Glad to hear it," his friend replied. "Because we need *your* help."

Jackson's brows arched upward. "My help?" Something told him he didn't want to hear what the other man had to say.

"I'm not going to be able to be there for my sister and her son right now," he said, and Jackson could tell it was tearing him apart. "At least, not like I'd planned to be. But I'm hoping they'll be able to have the next best thing—you."

Me? he thought, feeling the urge to back himself right out of Justin's office. The last thing Lainie wanted to do was spend time around him. "Justin, you know I would do anything for you. But how am I supposed to help Lainie with her son?"

"You're an uncle," his friend explained. "You've had experience with kids."

"Limited," he countered.

"More than me," Justin pointed out, effectively winning the debate.

"Have you forgotten about my bad leg?"

Justin arched a brow. "You can't be serious."

He was. But not because it would keep him from doing things with Justin's nephew. It was having Lainie see him limp around on his damaged leg, knowing he could never be the man she'd once been so determined to give her heart to.

"Look," his friend said, his tone serious, "if you're too busy to help me out, or would just prefer not to, just say so. I'll figure something out. I know you've just finished up the rodeo season and you're probably worn thin."

True. He was still recovering from spending weeks

on end, traveling from state to state with the broncs he and his brothers had contracted out to various rodeos. But this was his best friend asking for his help. More importantly, Lainie needed it, even if he was fairly certain she wouldn't want it. And Justin had enough on his plate as it was. He shouldn't have to be worrying about his sister as well.

Shoving his own reservations back, Jackson said with a sigh of resignation, "No need to look elsewhere. I'll do it."

Relief swept over the sheriff's face in the form of a wide smile. "Thanks. I owe you one. My sister's happiness means the world to me."

It meant the world to him, too, but Jackson wasn't so sure Lainie knew that. Probably for the best, he decided, because they could never go back to the way things were before he'd broken her heart.

Chapter Two

❧

"Morning," Lainie said in greeting as her brother, finally coming in from the night shift he'd had to work, stepped into the kitchen. He was a sight for sore eyes after her trip home and a long, restless night, having cried herself to sleep the night before thanks to an emotional journey.

"Sis," Justin replied with an affectionate grin as he crossed the kitchen to where she stood at the stove frying up some bacon. He gave her a warm, welcoming bear hug and then released her as he took a step back. "I'm sorry I couldn't be here with you last night."

She shrugged. "Life doesn't always work out the way we plan for it to." She knew that better than anyone. "Besides, Lucas and I were both spent. We went to bed early. Thank you for keeping me updated though. Sounds like things are more than a little bit crazy at work for you right now." He'd called her the evening before to explain what had happened and to let her know he wouldn't be making it home that night. Then he had texted her that morning to let her know he was finally on his way home and couldn't wait to see her and his nephew.

"To say the least. Deputy Vance and I were trying to get some sort of temporary schedule worked out."

"I hate the thought of you having driven home after working the night shift," she said with a frown. "If only I could have helped you." But she hadn't driven since the night of the accident that killed Will. Didn't think she ever would again, which was why she intended to look for a place in town. Lucas would be able to walk to school and she would be able to get to the grocery store, pharmacy, even the doctor, whatever either of them might need.

"I was able to grab an hour or so of shut-eye in my office when Deputy Vance came in to relieve me. After that, I felt rested enough to make the short drive home."

"That makes me feel a little better," she told him. "As anxious as I was to see you, I'm glad you stayed and got some much-needed rest before coming home." She couldn't bear it if something happened to him, too.

"Some homecoming, huh?" he said with a frown.

"It was probably for the best," she admitted. "Lucas wasn't in the best of moods when we got here yesterday."

Justin settled back against the kitchen counter, arms crossed in a casual stance. "Jackson said you and Lucas had words."

Lainie turned her attention back to the pan of crispy bacon atop the stove, a knot forming in her stomach. Just as she had feared, Jackson had been there long enough to hear at least part of the argument she was having with her son. "I wish you hadn't sent him here with the key."

"You'd rather I left you standing outside in the cold?"

She frowned. "No."

"You told me you wanted to wait until today to surprise Mom and Dad since you arrived early, and because you wanted to give Lucas a chance to settle in after the move. Therefore, my calling them to run over to Bent Creek to bring you their spare key was out of the question. So Jackson was the next-best thing."

Lainie sighed. "I'm sorry, Justin. I don't mean to give you a hard time. Especially since you're doing so much for Lucas and me, allowing us to stay here until we find a place of our own. But things are just…well, they're awkward between Jackson and myself." She'd also need to look for a job. While her husband had left them financially secure, she wanted to keep most of that money in the bank for unexpected expenses and for a college fund for her son.

He nodded in understanding. "I'd imagine they would be. You haven't really seen him or even spoken to him for years. What I don't understand is why that is."

Lainie prayed to the Lord for the emotional strength this homecoming was going to require of her. But if it helped her son, she would endure anything that came her way—even her foolish young past where she'd thrown herself, heart included, at Jackson, only to be told he didn't feel the same way.

"Life changes and so do people," she explained as she turned to the stove and began plucking the bacon out of the cast-iron frying pan with the tongs. She then placed the crispy strips onto the paper-towel-covered plate she'd put on the counter beside the stove. "Jackson is all about the rodeo," she went on, praying the hurt she'd tried to keep bottled up where her brother's best friend was concerned would remain where she'd placed it—buried deep. "And, of course, his family. Just as I'm not the same young girl who left Bent Creek all those years ago. I've grown up." *Grown wiser.* "The focus in my life is on my family, too, but most especially on my son. And now, more than ever, it needs to stay that way. I can't afford any distractions."

"Okay, so if I were to read a little deeper between the lines of that explanation, I think what you're also saying is that you still haven't gotten over Jackson," her brother said, taking Lainie by surprise.

Her head snapped around, her gaze meeting his. "Excuse me?"

Justin grabbed a cup from the kitchen cupboard and poured himself some of the coffee Lainie had made when she'd first awoken that morning. "When you were little," he said calmly, "you used to adore Jackson, following us around like a pesky shadow. As you got older, I would watch your face light up whenever he came over to visit."

"He was like my other brother," she said, realizing as soon as she'd said it that she'd done so a little too defensively. "I was always happy to see you when you came home."

"Maybe so," he conceded. "But I never got as many meatballs as you served Jackson with his spaghetti when you helped Mom with dinner. And I might also point out that his garlic bread slices were—"

"All right," she muttered as she placed the final bacon strip onto the awaiting plate and then turned to face him. "I might have had a small crush on your best friend. But I was young and foolish, and I can guarantee you that I'll never be that doe-eyed girl again where Jackson Wade is concerned."

"Never is a very long time," he pointed out.

"It's how it has to be."

"That being the case, do you think you could handle Jackson's stepping in for me where Lucas is concerned?"

"What are you talking about?"

"I asked Jackson to help you with Lucas until I get this mess at work straightened out."

"Justin," she groaned.

"He knows his way around kids," her brother hastened to explain.

She snorted. "Jackson Wade? The only thing he knows his way around is horses."

Her brother shook his head. "Not true. He has a niece, who is only a year or so younger than Lucas, and now two nephews, since Autumn recently gave birth, giving Tucker a son."

"But no children of his own," she countered.

"Neither do I, but you asked for my help with Lucas."

"That's different. And you are every bit as qualified as Jackson is as far as that goes. You have a nephew, too."

"Lainie," he said, sounding frustrated, "you know what I mean. However, the point I'm trying to make is that Jackson is a very devoted uncle who puts a good bit of time in with his niece and nephews. And the truth of the matter is that no man is born a father. That sort of thing comes later, with maturity and time. While Jackson and I aren't anyone's fathers yet, we are men.

We know what it's like to be a young boy. We know how their minds think, and what activities they like to participate in. Just give Jackson a chance."

Her brother might be right, but that didn't change things. She still reacted like a silly, lovestruck teenager whenever Jackson was near. To the point she felt like she was being disloyal to her husband.

"Lucas will be fine until you can spend time with him. I don't want or need Jackson's help. But please thank him for offering to do so the next time you see him. Once Christmas break is over, Lucas will be able to start making friends, which should help him settle into his new life here."

His worried frown deepened. "It's your decision. But that won't change the fact that you will be seeing Jackson from time to time."

She knew that. She couldn't ask her brother to keep Jackson from stopping by to see him. Nor would she. She would simply have to do her best to work around the situation whenever it occurred. Like go to her room and lose herself in a good book. Or even slip outside for a long walk.

"I'm an adult," she told him. "I think I can handle crossing paths with Jackson Wade from time to time." At least, she prayed she could.

"I'm glad to hear that," he replied. "Because the last thing I want to do is add to the stress you're under right now."

"I appreciate your concern," she told him as she pulled a carton from the fridge. "But I'm a lot stronger than I look. One or two eggs?"

He looked to the stove. "You don't have to cook for me."

"I want to." It made her feel like she was needed. Without Will in her life, and with her son pushing her away, Lainie felt like she was adrift in a churning sea of loneliness. It was her own fault. After the accident, she'd turned all her focus to Lucas, leaving no time for social interaction with the friends she'd made after she and Will had married. "How many eggs would you like? I just finished frying up the bacon right before you got home."

"Have you eaten?"

She shook her head. "No. But I'm not very hungry."

"Lainie, you need to eat," he insisted.

"Fine," she said, not having the energy to argue. "I'll have an egg, too."

"And Lucas?"

"He's still asleep. Traveling home yesterday took a lot out of him." As did his determination to fight this move, to fight her, she thought wearily, her heart aching. She turned back to the stove before her brother noticed the tears filling her eyes. While she had come there, praying her brother might be able to help her son, she didn't want to add to Justin's stress at that moment. Not with all he had going on at work. She could weather this storm a little longer on her own, just as she had been for the past eight months or so, ever since her son had started acting out with fits of anger. "How many eggs would you like?" she called back over her shoulder.

"Two, please."

"Over easy with a dash of pepper?"

"I can't believe you remember that."

She remembered a lot of things. Some she wished she didn't. Like the kiss she had given her brother's best friend at the Old West Festival Dance, one that had every bit of her heart behind it, and then the rejection that had followed. She remembered her determination to forget him, and then her rush to find the kind of love Jackson had denied her.

Will had been the one to give her that love. While he hadn't taken Jackson's place completely, it had been enough for her to find happiness with her husband, even have a son with him. She also remembered arguing with him before driving home from the cocktail party his company had given in his honor for landing one of the biggest contracts their firm had ever closed on. She'd been upset with him for partaking in far too many celebratory toasts. And to think she'd appointed herself his designated driver, to make certain they both got home safely, only to be hit by another driver who hadn't let someone else take him home. She would never forget the jarring impact of the other car slamming into them, followed by pain and fear as the darkness had engulfed her.

"Lainie?" Her brother's worried voice brought her back to the present. She shoved the painful memories away and forced a smile as she carried the egg carton over to the counter by the stove. "Toast?" she asked as she cracked an egg over the nonstick frying pan she had set out on the burner next to the cast-iron skillet.

"Sounds good," Justin said. "But I'm fixing it for us."

She nodded and watched as her brother crossed the kitchen to the pantry. "When do you have to go back to work?"

"This afternoon," he replied as he returned with a

half-eaten loaf of bread. "After I get a few more hours of sleep."

"Oh," she replied, her shoulders sagging. She thought they'd have at least a little time to spend together before his next shift. It looked as if her parents were going to have to come to her and Lucas instead.

Her brother stepped over and wrapped a supportive arm around her shoulders. "I really am sorry, sis. I know this isn't working out the way we planned, but everything's going to be all right. I promise."

He had always been a man of his word. But it was a promise she wasn't sure he'd be able to keep. Her life felt like it had unraveled at its seams to the point no amount of sewing would ever be able to repair it. No matter how many prayers she sent heavenward. All she could do was nod her reply.

"You look great by the way," he said, his tone more uplifting.

Lainie snorted as her gaze met his. Then she poked a finger into his shirt, nudging him away. "I'd appreciate it if you would take a step or two back, so your nose doesn't poke my eye out when it starts to grow."

"I'm not lying," he said with a chuckle. "Considering all you've been dealing with, you look good."

"Well, you don't," she countered.

Justin's dark brows lifted.

"It's the truth," she said, managing a small grin. "You look like you just rolled out of bed fully dressed." Her gaze moved down to his wrinkled uniform and then back up to his face. "And you need a shave."

Her brother chuckled. "I did just roll out of bed, or off my office sofa to be exact." He scrubbed a hand down over his jaw. "I was on my way to grab a shower and shave when I heard someone moving about in the kitchen. I figured you'd be sleeping in, too."

"I couldn't," she admitted. "Too much on my mind I suppose."

His expression sobered. "I hate that you've had to deal with everything on your own. Especially over the holidays."

"It was my choice," she reminded him, not wanting to think about Christmas being only a couple of weeks away.

The doorbell rang, thankfully taking her brother's focus off her problems. "Be right back."

Lainie watched him go and then turned back to the stove. Grabbing the shaker, she sprinkled some salt over the eggs and added a dash of pepper. Then, reaching for the spatula, she flipped them over in the pan.

"Morning," a husky male voice, not her brother's, said from the entryway behind her.

Her eyes widened, and her foolish heart immediately sped up. She cast an anxious glance back over her shoulder to find Jackson Wade standing there, cowboy hat held in one hand, looking every bit as uncomfortable as she felt.

"Morning," she replied.

Justin stepped past him into the kitchen. "Come on in," he told his friend. "We're just getting ready to have some breakfast. You hungry?"

"No," Jackson answered. "I ran into Deputy Vance when I stopped by Abby's to grab a doughnut and a cup of coffee this morning. He said you'd gone home to catch up on some much-needed sleep."

Lainie turned to look at the two men. "I could step out of the room if you need to talk to Justin."

Jackson shook his head. "No need. I just came by to see what time I was supposed to pick you up and take you to your mom and dad's today."

"You could have called," Justin noted. "Saved yourself a trip over here."

Jackson's brows drew together. "I don't have Lainie's number and I figured you were fast asleep. It wasn't like I had to go out of my way to swing by here. We are neighbors, you know."

Lainie was still trying to process Jackson's reason for being there. "Justin asked *you* to take Lucas and me to Mom and Dad's?"

"I did," her brother said matter-of-factly as he removed the nylon spatula from her hand and then nudged her aside.

Only then did Lainie realize the eggs she'd been making them for breakfast had started to burn, all thanks to their unexpected visitor.

"When I knew I wouldn't be free to take you to see them," her brother explained, somewhat apologetically as he slid the crispy-edged eggs out onto the awaiting plates, "I called Jackson to see if he could run you over there."

"He doesn't need to do that," Lainie insisted with a frown, her gaze fixed on Jackson's handsome face.

"You can't walk there," her brother pointed out. "And you need to go see Mom and Dad before they catch wind of your being here ahead of schedule."

"She could take your truck," Jackson suggested.

Her brother shook his head. "Lainie doesn't drive anymore or I would have offered it to her."

Jackson's gaze swung back her way, surprise registering on his face. But he didn't press her with questions. Instead, he said, "It's a short ride. I'll drop you off at your parents' place and then go home. You can give me a call when you're ready for me to pick you and Lucas up." He looked even less happy about the situation than she did.

Of course, that shouldn't surprise her. Jackson had effectively rid himself of her all those years ago. She was quite certain he wasn't the least bit eager to have her shoved back into his life again. But she wanted to see her parents, enough to go along with her brother's alternative plan—Jackson included.

"Lainie!" her mother squealed in delight the second she opened the door and saw her daughter standing there. Her gaze dropped down to her grandson, her happiness at seeing him written all over her face. "Lucas! Look how big you've gotten since we saw you last!" She bent to capture him in a warm hug.

Lainie waited, fearing her son's response, because he'd been avoiding any sort of affection where Lainie was concerned. But he reciprocated his grandmother's warm embrace and then stood smiling while she planted several happy kisses on his cheeks. Lainie felt both relief and hurt.

Her mother leaned in to give Lainie a loving hug as well. "We didn't expect you home until tomorrow."

"We got an earlier start than we had planned." She left out the part where her son had threatened to run away so he wouldn't have to leave his dad. Lainie had tried to explain to Lucas that his father would be with him anywhere he went, that his soul was no longer with his body where it had been laid to rest, but with the Lord. When he hadn't seemed accepting of her gentle explanation, she'd decided not to wait to go home to Bent Creek. It hadn't been cheap to change their flights last minute, but the relief she'd felt when they'd landed in Rock Springs, Wyoming, so close to home and the help she so badly needed, was worth the cost.

"Well, come on in," her mother said, stepping aside as she motioned them into the one-bedroom, ground floor condo her parents had moved into a little over four years earlier. Her father's arthritic knees had pained him too much going up and down the stairs in the home Lainie and Justin had been raised in. So her parents had downsized into a much more manageable one-story condo a town over from Bent Creek, selling their house to Justin for far less than they could have gotten for it on the open housing market. But that's how her parents had always been—striving to make her and Justin's lives better any way they could.

"Baby girl!" her father said as he joined them in the entryway.

"Dad," she said, stepping into his welcoming embrace.

Her father turned to Lucas. "And who's this young man?" He pretended to search beyond her son. "Where's my baby boy?"

Lucas groaned. "Grandpa."

Her father's eyes widened. "Lucas? Is that really you?"

Her mother gave her husband a nudge. "Stop your teasing. We both know we can't keep him our little boy forever."

If only that were possible, Lainie thought sadly. Lucas had always adored her. That's why this change in him was so heartbreaking.

"Afternoon, Jackson," her father said, glancing past Lainie and her son.

Jackson gave a nod in greeting. "Mr. Dawson." Then he looked to her mother. "Mrs. Dawson."

Her mother smiled. "It's so good to see you." Her gaze moved beyond him. "Where's Justin?"

"Home, catching up on his sleep," Lainie explained. "He worked the night shift last night and has to go back in later this afternoon."

Disappointment registered on her mother's face. "That son of mine is always burning the candle at both ends." She looked to Jackson. "Well, come on in out of that cold."

"I'm not staying," he told her. "Just dropping Lainie and Lucas off."

"Don't be silly," the older woman said with a wave of her hand. "There's no sense in you making two trips out here. Stay and visit."

He hesitated, looking uncomfortable. "This is family time. You don't need me around while you're catching up with your daughter and your grandson."

"You are family," her father said with a warm smile.

"That's right," Lainie's mother said. "You are. Now come on inside. It's cold out."

Jackson looked to Lainie for help, but if she were to put up any sort of protest it would have her parents asking questions she'd rather not have to answer. So he nodded his consent, swept the cowboy hat from his head and stepped the rest of the way inside, closing the door behind him.

"Lucas, there's a plate of Christmas cookies on the kitchen table," her mother said. "Grandma baked them this morning if you'd like to go pick a few out."

Lucas's face lit up and then her son raced off in search of the sugary sweets his grandmother had no doubt prepared for his arrival.

"Two cookies!" Lainie hollered after him, knowing full well her son would go for the iced cut-out sugar cookies. They were his favorite. And her mother's tended to be the size of cereal bowls.

"I thought your brother told me he was off today," her mother said as she led them into the living room.

"He was supposed to be," Lainie replied as she removed her coat and draped it over the arm of the sofa.

"Deputy Culler fell off a ladder while putting up Christmas lights and had to be taken to the hospital," Jackson explained further. "Justin had to cover for him last night."

Her mother's hand went to her mouth. "Oh, that poor man," she groaned in sympathy. "Is he all right?"

"He fractured his hip and had to have emergency surgery," he explained. "But he'll be fine."

"Thank the Lord it wasn't worse," her father said. "He could've broken his neck."

Like Will had when the car driven by a very intoxicated teenage boy struck ours. Lainie felt nausea stir in the pit of her stomach.

"Oh, honey," her dad said, his face blanching as he realized what he'd just said. "I didn't mean to stir up old—"

"It's okay, Dad," she said, hurrying to cut him off. Her son didn't know any of the details about his father's passing, other than the fact that she had been behind the wheel when the accident had occurred. And he only knew that because one of his friends at school had overheard his mother talking to another mother about Lucas's father's accident. That came after a more recent incident in their community that also involved a teen driving recklessly. Thankfully, the other driver's quick reactions had allowed him to steer clear of what could have been a truly serious outcome—like it had been with her and Will.

Pulling herself together, as she'd had to do since that night she'd awakened in the hospital to find out her husband hadn't survived the wreck, she said, "I agree. Deputy Culler was very blessed to have come out of it with only a broken hip. But that means Justin and Deputy Vance are going to be handling all the shifts until he can bring in some backup." She was shocked to sound so calm when so much guilt and regret was whirling about inside her.

"What about Deputy Mitchell?" her father asked.

"Apparently, Deputy Mitchell is on a cruise in Alaska somewhere."

"Poor Justin," her mother said with a worried frown. "He works himself to the bone as it is. And poor Kathy. She's got to be beside herself with worry. A broken hip will mean a long recovery for Todd. I'll have to make some soup and corn bread to take over to the Cullers after he gets home. Kathy will no doubt have her hands full taking care of her husband."

Lainie smiled. So like her mom, always caring about others. "I'm sure they would appreciate that."

"I think I'll go peek in on my grandson," her dad said, getting up from his seat. "Wouldn't want him to spoil his appetite."

Her mother laughed as he walked away. "Same goes for you," she called after him and then turned back to

Lainie and Jackson. "Your father is going to be a bad influence on your son, I'm afraid."

"A little sugar won't hurt him, I suppose," Lainie replied with a shrug. She had learned not to sweat the small stuff. She had much bigger stuff in her life to contend with.

"You should know," her mother said with a smile. "Your father 'snuck' you and your brother plenty of sweets when the two of you were growing up."

"And I loved him for it." And she loved him for giving her and Justin a place to call home. For making them feel safe and loved. The humor left her eyes. "How's Dad doing? He's not moving around as well as he was the last time I saw him." That had been the previous December, when her parents and Justin had flown to Sacramento the week before Christmas to spend a few days with her and Lucas, because she couldn't bring herself to come home for the holidays. Guilt at Will's passing still kept her from wanting to celebrate anything. She'd only done so for her son's sake, wanting to keep his life as normal as possible.

Her mother gave a wave of her hand. "Don't go worrying yourself over us. Your father and I are doing fine. Just the aches and pains that come along with getting old." She leaned forward, placing a hand on Lainie's knee. "The question is, how are *you* doing, honey?"

Lainie shot a nervous glance in Jackson's direction, praying he wouldn't bring up the argument he'd witnessed between her and her son, and then turned to smile at her mother. "I'm home where all my family and friends are. How could I not be happy?"

"We're so glad to have you back here with us," her

mother said, tearing up. "It makes me want to move back to Bent Creek."

"I'm sure Justin would be more than willing to sell the house back to you and Dad. But keep in mind that he loves that place, which means you'll more than likely be stuck with him living there with the two of you."

Her mother laughed. "He does love the ranch. So did we. But this condo works best with your father's physical limitations. Not that I wouldn't love having both you and your brother and my grandson, living under the same roof as us again."

"That would be nice," Lainie concurred. "But as much as I would like to go back to the way things were, I know better. We can't turn back time. All we can do is move on and accept the fact that nothing stays the same."

"I beg to differ," Jackson said, meeting her gaze. "Some things do remain the same."

Lainie stiffened. As if she didn't already know where his feelings lay where she was concerned. "Another reason not to look back, but to move on."

Her mother's confused gaze shifted back and forth between Lainie and Jackson. "Well," she said, as if sensing there was more to the conversation than what she was hearing, "one thing that hasn't changed is the happiness it brings me to have you home for the holidays. And, Jackson, plan on joining us at Justin's place for Christmas Eve lunch. It'll be just like old times." Her brows drew together in worry. "Unless that would interfere with plans you have with your ever-growing family."

He looked to Lainie, who was mentally begging him

to refuse her mother's invitation, and then nodded. "I'd like that, Mrs. Dawson. What can I bring?"

What could he bring? Lainie looked at Jackson in disbelief. He really intended to come to their holiday gathering?

"Just bring yourself," her mother said happily. "I'm sure you and Lainie have a lot of catching up to do."

"Not really," Lainie countered. "Justin has kept me up-to-date on Jackson and his rodeo company's pursuits."

Jackson's dark brows lifted, as did the corner of his mouth with her pronouncement. Then that Wade dimple worked its way to the surface. "Keeping tabs on me, Lainie?"

Heat crept up her neck. Pushing up from the sofa, Lainie turned to her mom. "I'm going to go check in on Lucas and Dad and make sure they haven't eaten all your cookies."

"Be sure to bring one back for Jackson, honey," her mother called after her. "You know how much he always liked my sugar cookies."

Far more than he'd ever liked her, Lainie thought with a frown as she hurried away. And she would do well to remember that.

Chapter Three

"You cutting out for the day?"

Jackson released his hold on his truck's door handle and turned to see one of his brothers, Garrett, leaning against the open barn door, concern written across his face. His other brother, Tucker, stood next to him, his mouth drawn in a tight line.

"I've got an errand to run."

"Everything okay?" Tucker asked with a studying glance.

Of course his brothers would pick up on his being a little off his game, despite Jackson's efforts to go on as he always had. Not an easy task when inside his thoughts were whirling around like crazy, dragging his emotions right along with them.

Sighing, Jackson said, "I'm on my way out to Justin's place."

"I think you'll have better luck finding him in town," Tucker said. "That man never stops working. Especially now that Deputy Culler is laid up."

"I'm not going over to his place to see him," Jackson confessed. "I'm going over to check on Lainie and her son."

Simultaneously, his brothers' eyes rounded, making them look like a couple of startled hoot owls.

"Lainie?" Garrett repeated in confusion.

"She's home?" Tucker said in surprise.

Jackson nodded. "She and her son flew in the day before last."

"That so?" Garrett said as he peeled off his work gloves, shoving them into the back pocket of his jeans. "You never made any mention of it."

"I couldn't," Jackson replied. "I gave my word to Justin to keep it to myself until Lainie could get out to visit with her parents. She came home sooner than expected and wanted to surprise them, which she did yesterday."

"Yesterday?" Tucker repeated. "So it's no longer a secret that she's home, yet you still kept it to yourself? You know Mom would want to know Lainie's back. Especially now that it's for good. They always get together when she comes home."

Yes, they did find time to meet up when Lainie came home. His mother would always give them the rundown of what was new with Lainie after every visit, since Jackson and his brothers were usually out of town when she came to Bent Creek to see her family. It was him Lainie clearly didn't want anything to do with, strategically planning her visits around his not being there. Her determination to avoid him because of the hurt he'd caused her was something he prayed he would be able to set to rights—even though he knew there was no chance of anything more than friendship between them. Not only because Lainie had moved on a long time ago, but because he was no longer the man she had been starry-eyed over. He was a has-been rodeo champ with a lame leg. But if she was going to be putting down roots again in Bent Creek with her son, they needed to find some way to coexist without the past coming between them.

"Never mind that," Tucker said, drawing Jackson from his thoughts. "Are you really going over to Jackson's to check up on Lainie and her son?"

He nodded.

"To make amends with her?" Garrett pressed.

His brother's words caught Jackson off guard. "Amends for what?" he heard himself say.

"Maybe it's time you tell us," Garrett said. "You and Lainie used to be so close. And then she went off to school and everything changed. It was as if she had shut you out of her life. And she only came home to visit when you weren't here. And if you were, she deliberately steered clear of you."

"Garrett's right," Tucker said with a nod of agreement. "There was no missing the divide that had fallen between the two of you more than a decade ago. Only we never understood why."

"What happened between the two of you?" Garrett asked. "Lainie was the sister we all longed to have after losing ours, but she was even closer to you considering all the time you spent over at the Dawsons' with Justin when we were growing up."

"She wasn't like a sister to me," he countered with a growl of frustration. He'd given up so much when he'd let her go. Something that had only really set in the day she'd called to tell him she was getting married. "At least, not as we grew older."

His brothers exchanged glances before turning their focus back to Jackson.

"Care to explain?" Garrett said, his request tendered without the usual teasing that went on between the three of them.

Jackson looked down at the thin coating of snow that covered the ground around his booted feet. He'd never lied to his family when directly asked a question and he wasn't about to start now.

"I don't know how it happened," he began honestly, lifting his gaze to meet theirs. "Lainie was Justin's little sister. But as time went on and we got older, I started noticing her as the pretty, kindhearted young woman she was growing up to be. But I forced myself to think of her as Justin's baby sister, not as just Lainie. That all changed when she kissed me," he said, telling them what he hadn't told anyone, not even his best friend, for all those years.

"Lainie kissed you?" Tucker exclaimed in surprise.

Garrett elbowed him in the ribs. "Let him finish."

"Sorry," he apologized. "Go on."

"It might have started out that way, but then I found myself kissing her back," Jackson admitted. "It was at the Old West Festival Dance after she graduated from high school. Before she went off to college and I went off to ride the rodeo circuit."

"And you were such a bad kisser that she's spent the years since trying to avoid you?" Tucker said, only to receive chastising scowls from both Garrett and Jackson.

Tucker shrugged. "Sorry, just trying to lighten the mood. I can tell what happened back then still weighs pretty heavy on your heart."

"It does," he said. They had no idea just how heavy. "Lainie wanted to see where things might go between us. Even going so far as to tell me she was willing to

turn down her full ride to college in California to remain in Bent Creek near me. Said she would find a
job that would allow her to switch up her work schedule to travel to the rodeos I would be competing in."
Jackson's pained frown deepened. "I couldn't let her
do that, sacrifice all the hard work she had put into getting that academic scholarship for me. So I told her that
I only thought of her as a little sister. Nothing more.
That the rodeo was where my heart lay. Or something
to that effect."

"Ouch," Tucker said. "No wonder she has been
avoiding you."

"You did the right thing," Garrett said with a nod.

Had he? Jackson wondered. Because letting Lainie
go had been the biggest regret of his life.

Jackson caught sight of Lainie's son slipping into the
fort at the edge of the tree line as he drove up to Justin's place. He couldn't help but wonder if Lucas and
his mother had gotten into another argument like the
one he'd happened upon the day she'd arrived in Bent
Creek. He prayed not. It had hurt his heart to see the
emotional divide between the two of them.

He thanked the Lord, as he was sure Lainie had, that
her parents hadn't seemed to notice the rift between
mother and son when Jackson had taken them there to
visit. But then the Dawsons were overcome with joy
to have them both back in Wyoming for good. Lucas
had chatted away with his grandparents as if nothing
was amiss, had feasted on the cookies his grandmother
had baked for him, had even smiled, but every time
Lainie had attempted to be a part of her son's conversation with his grandparents he'd either clammed up or

responded with his tiny brows knitted tightly together in an angry scowl.

Shutting off the engine, Jackson stepped down from his truck and made his way around to the back of the house. Sure enough, Lucas was exactly where Jackson had expected him to be, seated inside the fort on the rough-hewn wooden bench that ran along one side of the small space. Leaning back against the rows of treated boards that made up the walls, Lucas sat with his arms crossed, bottom lip trembling, tears spilling from his closed eyes.

Jackson knocked at the entrance where Lucas had left the door partially open in his haste to get inside.

The boy jumped, his head snapping up. "M-Mr. Wade," he choked out.

Removing his cowboy hat, Jackson ducked and stepped inside. "Seems like I'm not the only one who thought this looked like a good place to slip away to and do some thinking," he said matter-of-factly as he settled his much-larger frame onto the bench next to Lucas.

"I'm not thinking," Lainie's son said with a sniffle.

"No? Because this fort is the kind of place men tend to slip away to when they've got things on their mind that need to be sorted out."

"But I'm not a man," he countered.

"You're not too far off from becoming one," Jackson told him.

Lucas straightened ever so slightly, as if trying to appear the young man Jackson proclaimed him to be.

"Mind if I sit here and do some thinking, too?" Jackson glanced around as if taking in his surroundings. "Seems like a good place to do some."

The boy shrugged. "I suppose."

"I'll just sit here, real quiet-like, while I mull some things over." Like what he was supposed to do next. Coloring with his niece was one thing. Dealing with a little boy so overwhelmed by grief and anger over the death of his father that he couldn't contain his emotions was a whole different matter altogether. "Unless you feel the need to talk," he added as he placed his cowboy hat on the bench beside him and leaned back against the winter-chilled wall, crossing his arms in imitation of the distraught young man beside him.

Silence filled the small, five-by-six fort for several minutes. Jackson had to wonder if the cold was getting to Lucas like it was to him, seeping in through the thick denim of his jeans. It was December, after all.

"I wasn't crying," he said defensively. "Because men don't cry. I was just thinking really hard."

"Men do cry, son," he told him. "My father cried when my mom was really sick. My brother Tucker cried when he and his wife had their baby boy." He'd cried the day Lainie wed, he thought, the pain of it feeling as if it had just happened. No one had seen him do so, of course. It would only have led to questions he'd just as soon not have to answer. Questions like the ones he'd answered before leaving the ranch to go check on Lainie and her son.

"I cried when my dad died."

"Understandable," Jackson said quietly.

"And when my mom said we had to move away." Scuffing the heel of one of his booted feet atop the floorboards, Lucas added with a mutter, "I don't like it here."

Jackson took a moment before responding, wanting to gather his thoughts. "No shame in feeling the way you do," he finally said. "A move is a big thing, saying goodbye to old friends and all. But it also brings new friends into your life. New opportunities. And you might hold off passing judgment on Bent Creek until you've had a chance to really see what living here is like." He prayed both Lucas and Lainie would find the happiness they were seeking here in Bent Creek.

"I want everything to be the way it used to be," Lucas said, a small sob escaping his lips.

He couldn't put himself in Lainie's son's shoes where the move was concerned. He'd lived his whole life in Bent Creek. But he did know a thing or two about grief. The hurt from losing his little sister still ran deep. He couldn't even imagine what it felt like to be Lucas's age and lose a father.

Jackson looked to Lainie's little boy, who looked so much like his mother, from his dark brown hair to the slight sprinkling of freckles across the bridge of his nose. "Change can be hard," he admitted. "Sometimes painfully so." Especially when that change had involved hurting Lainie all those years ago, something she had never forgiven him for. But her happiness had meant the world to him, still did, in fact, and he knew that if she had given up the opportunity for him, Lainie would have come to resent him for it. So he'd done the only thing he could—he'd shut her out emotionally. The hurt he'd seen on her face that night, hurt he'd put there, had nearly broken him. He'd hoped that someday, once she'd finished college, he and Lainie might be at a better place to see where things might go between them. Only Lainie had moved on, finding the love he'd denied her, much to his regret. When she'd called to tell him that she had gotten engaged, it sent his entire life into a complete tailspin. And he had no one to blame but himself for his heart's loss. "I can tell you this," he added with a gentle smile. "Your mom wants you to be happy more than anything in the world. That's why she brought you back to the place she grew up in, where you will have family and new friends." He glanced up. "And this really cool fort."

"Lucas!" Lainie's voice rang out. A second later, the fort's door squeaked open and she appeared in the undersized doorway. Her reddened eyes told Jackson that, like her son, she'd been crying, too. "Jackson?" she gasped in surprise, an immediate frown pulling at her pink lips.

He stood so abruptly, he struck the top of his head on the low-hanging ceiling—one meant for children, not full-grown men—with a loud thwack. "Lainie," he replied with a grimace. Looking down into her pretty, tear-streaked face, his heart went out to her. He understood the tension he'd felt between her and her son a little better. Lucas was clearly struggling with being uprooted and he blamed his mother, who was doing what she felt best for him.

Worry pulled at Lainie's features as her gaze zeroed in on the top of his head. "Jackson," she said with a fretful groan. "Are you all right?" she asked, her hand lifting as if to see for herself. But then she drew back, letting her hand fall back down to her side.

Something sparked inside of him at that small gesture of concern, even if she had caught herself before acting upon it. It told him that a part of Lainie still cared about him, despite her determination to have him believe otherwise. Jackson rubbed the tender spot on the crown of his head as he hunkered just low enough to avoid any more contact with the wood planks above. "If this skull can take hitting a dirt-packed rodeo arena floor after getting bucked off a couple-thousand-pound bull, a little bump on the noggin isn't going to do much harm."

Contrary to the nod she gave him, the sadness in her hazel eyes seemed to deepen. Not that he would have thought that even possible. It was then Jackson realized he'd brought up the one thing that had put a wedge between them all those years ago, at least in her mind—his rodeo career. His heart suddenly felt like it was lodged in his gut. He hadn't meant to bring up something that would only serve to add to her emotional hurts.

Memories of that evening, of the special dance they'd shared outside in the moonlight and all that had followed, came rushing to the surface of his mind. The choice he'd had to make that night had changed their relationship irrevocably, but he'd done it for Lainie. *I love you,* she'd said. And then he'd broken her heart. He'd never forget the intense regret that filled him at that moment, or the effort it took not to pull her back into his arms and tell her that he loved her, too. Instead, he'd stood silent, watching as Lainie lifted her chin, and then turned and walked away, out of his life without another word. His brave, sweet Lainie. *No, not his*, Jackson had to remind himself. He'd thrown that chance away a long time ago.

"What are you doing here?" she demanded, bringing Jackson back from his troubled thoughts.

He glanced back at her son. "Lucas and I were just sitting here, doing some thinking."

Lucas nodded in agreement, keeping his gaze firmly averted from his mother. "It's what men do," her son told her, his arms still crossed in front of him.

"I just wanted to let you know that lunch is ready," she said, the tension between them thick in the air.

That had Jackson's own frown deepening. His gaze swung back around to Lainie. "Would it be all right if Lucas and I took a couple more minutes to mull *life* over?"

She bit at her bottom lip in indecision and then nodded. "But not too long. It's cold out."

"I have my coat and gloves on," her son pointed out. "And Mr. Wade and me are men. We don't get cold."

Lainie offered up a soft smile. "I suppose you are. But lunch won't stay warm for long."

"He'll be right in," Jackson said, making the decision for Lucas, whose chin lifted in a way that reminded him so much of Lainie. "Wouldn't want to waste a good meal."

"Can Jackson eat lunch with us?" Lucas asked, his request taking Jackson by surprise.

"Sweetie, I don't think—"

"That's okay. I really should get going," Jackson cut in, saving Lainie from having to refuse her son's unexpected request, which he knew she would have. Lainie hadn't avoided him for so many years only to come home and invite him to lunch. He should have considered that before giving his friend his promise to help out. In doing Justin a favor, he was putting Lainie in an uncomfortable position. But Lucas needed help finding his way back to the carefree, happy path in life every child deserved to travel. Jackson knew at that moment, as he stood between two people in great pain, people he cared a great deal about, that he would do anything he could, no matter how big or how small, to help make things right.

"Please stay," Lucas pleaded, and then finally looked to his mother. "It's okay, isn't it?"

She smiled again, but Jackson was pretty sure it was

only for her son's benefit. "You're here," she told Jackson. "You might as well stay for a bite to eat."

Jackson returned her grin, offering up a charming one of his own. "Well, all right then." Looking to Lucas, he said, "Looks like I'll be staying."

"Okay, then," Lainie said. "While the two of you finish 'mulling' things over, I'll go inside and set another place at the table." Before either of them had a chance to respond, she was gone.

Jackson was still staring at the empty doorway when Lucas said, "I didn't really like it in California either. Not anymore."

Understandable, Jackson thought. California had to hold some very painful memories for him with the loss of his father. "Well, I truly do hope you'll at least give Bent Creek a chance. I think you'll come to like living here," Jackson said as he settled his large frame back down onto the bench next to Lucas. "Bent Creek is a pretty special place to grow up in. I should know. I've been here all of my life. In fact, your mom and your uncle Justin and I have been friends since we were barely out of diapers."

"Were you friends with my dad, too?"

He shook his head. "Your dad wasn't from around here. Your mom met him when she was away at college." A twinge of jealousy pinched at his gut at the memory of that call he'd received from Lainie right before he was set to compete in the Vegas finals. A call that had not only ended his rodeo career, but any chance there might have been for the two of them to find their way back to each other.

"My mom doesn't talk about him anymore."

Jackson could hear the pain in Lucas's softly spoken words and his heart went out to him. He never expected to be discussing Lainie's love for another man with anyone, but at that moment it felt important to do so. "I would imagine it's hard for your mom to talk about him. She loved your dad. Just like you did."

Lord, please help me to find a way to help Lainie and her son in their time of need, Jackson thought as everything he'd just learned settled in.

"Thank you for lunch," Jackson said to Lainie later that afternoon. He cast a glance in her direction as she walked him outside, something she had insisted on doing when he'd announced it was time for him to take his leave.

"You're welcome," she replied, trying to push down all the old feelings being around Jackson again had stirred up and failing miserably. But she would fight it. For her son, who needed her attention focused solely on him. And for herself, because her heart was far too weary to take on any more hurt.

"Something on your mind?" he asked as they neared his truck.

Forcing herself to look up at him, into a face that had grown even more handsome with age, Lainie said, "I don't want you coming out here anymore. At least, not when Justin isn't here." She didn't want Jackson to witness any more friction between her and her son than he already had. Although surprisingly, during lunch her son had seemed more like the little boy he was before the accident, before his grief had surfaced and the anger had settled in. He'd been talking Jackson's ear off, asking him all about his ranch and his horses. And Lainie had to admit she'd been a little envious of Jackson for his ability to draw her son out of his shell in such a positive way, something she no longer seemed to be able to do.

He stopped walking, bringing her own steps to a halt as he turned to face her. "I'm here because your brother can't be."

"That's not his decision to make," she told him with a frown. "Lucas and I don't need a babysitter."

"I'm not a babysitter," he said with a tenderness that made her want to cry. "I'm here because my best friend asked me to be. Because I gave my word to Justin, something I stand by. And because no matter how you feel about me, I will always care about you. I want you and your son to be happy."

Jackson became a blur before her as hot tears pooled in her eyes. Lainie turned away. "I don't want you to care about me." She had only loved two men in her life. One had died because of her. The other had nearly died because of her. Not that anyone had ever put the blame for Jackson's rodeo-career-ending fall on her, but she knew the truth. Deep down, in her heart. She hadn't known he was in Vegas competing in the National Finals Rodeo when she'd called to tell him she was getting married. She didn't even know why she'd called him. She just had. She supposed that she'd wanted to let him know that someone had come along who wanted to spend their life with her. And there was still a very small part of her that wanted to see if her news sparked anything inside him. Lord forgive her for her actions. She'd had no right to care about Jackson's feelings for her, not when she was going to be marrying Will. Jackson had fallen silent for several heartbeats before finally congratulating her and wishing her all the happiness in the world. Happiness that he might have given her, had he loved her the way she had once loved him.

A gentle hand came to rest atop her shoulder and a small sob escaped her lips. "Lainie," Jackson said, empathy filling his husky voice.

She held up a staying hand. "Jackson, don't." Don't what she didn't know. She just couldn't do this. Not here. Not now.

His hand fell away. "All right," he said. "I accept that you don't want my help. Can barely stand to be around me. But I'm asking you to do this for your son. Let me help you get your little boy back."

Do this for your son. If he had said anything but that, she would have sent him away, holding firm to her resolve to keep Jackson Wade at a safe distance, both physically and emotionally. But he was right. Her moving home was about her son. Jackson's being there had sparked something positive in Lucas. Could the man who had crushed her tender heart so many years ago truly be the answer to her prayers where her son's happiness was concerned? It seemed there was only one way to find out, even if it meant risking the emotional pain all over again.

Chapter Four

"Am I forgiven yet?"

Lainie lowered the book she was reading, or at least trying to read as her mind kept drifting off to thoughts of Jackson. She met her brother's unapologetic grin from where he sat watching an NFL football game on his oversize flat-screen TV. "If you were truly remorseful for what you've done, then I might consider forgiving you. But we both know you're not."

"No," he said, his expression sobering. "I suppose I'm not. If I can't be there for you, then I need to know that you and Lucas are in good hands. Jackson is my best friend. I would trust him with my life. You could do the same."

Maybe so, she thought in silent response, *but what about my heart?* Not that there was any chance she was going to risk the hurt that came with loving someone ever again. She had loved Jackson and so naively thought he'd loved her, too. Maybe his feelings were not as deep as hers, but she had been so certain there was a spark of something that had flickered to life the year she was preparing to leave for college. Apparently, she had been wrong. And then came Will, who had been a comfortable fit, the kind of man born to be a husband and a father. Hardworking, loving and now gone because of her. She should be thinking of him whenever her thoughts drifted. Not Jackson.

"Lainie," her brother said with a sigh as he muted the game and shifted in the chair to face her, "I don't know what happened between you and Jackson to cause such a rift, but I do know that he cares about you. Always has."

The snort was out before she could think better of it. And, sure enough, her brother latched on to her far too honest reaction.

"This is exactly why the two of you need to talk. To work through whatever misunderstanding is responsible for putting this emotional distance between you and Jackson. Because if you think he doesn't care about you, you're wrong. After you'd gone off to school, and even later, after you'd married and started your family with Will, every time I mentioned speaking to you, he would ask me how you were doing. Even when he'd nearly died after that bull ground him into the arena floor, you were the first thing he spoke of when I went to visit him at the hospital. He said that all he wanted was for you to be happy and if Will was able to give you that then he wished you both well." His brows drew together in consternation before he added, "Although I'm not sure how he even knew about your engagement when we didn't even know about it at that point."

Lainie felt the hot surge of tears at her brother's words. Jackson knew because she had called to tell him. His rejection of her had allowed her to move down a new path in her life, where she found Will, a man willing to give his heart completely to her. If only she'd been able to give all of her heart to her husband. Emotions so raw and deep pushed upward, making it impossible to respond. Dropping the book she'd been reading onto her lap, she brought her hands up to cover her face as the first choked sob escaped.

"Lainie," her brother gasped. There was a loud clunk as he shoved the recliner's footrest closed and a second later he was seated next to her, holding her close. "I'm sorry. I never should have brought Will up."

She shook her head. "It's not that."

"Jackson?" he asked hesitantly.

"Yes," she said with a soft sniffle.

"I thought things were going well. You've spent time with him every day since coming home more than a week ago, even going with him over to his place. If I had known that bringing the two of you back together would make you this miserable, I never would have asked Jackson for his help. I'll talk to him tomorrow and let him know this isn't working out."

"That's the problem," she said with a sniffle. "It *is*."

Her brother loosened his hold on her and sat back, brows drawn together in confusion as he searched her face. "I don't understand."

"It is working," she told him. "Lucas is responding to Jackson where he never did with our preacher, his guidance counselor at school, even the therapist I took him to when I felt him slipping away. My son has interacted more positively with people in these past five days than he has with me for the past eight months, and most of that has been with Jackson. And you, of course." Not that her brother had been around much since their arrival, but she understood why that was.

He shook his head. "Then you're crying because you're happy?"

Lainie's shoulders sagged. Sighing, she dropped her gaze to the book in her lap, unable to look her brother in the eye as she said in a tight whisper, "I'm crying because I want to hold on to the anger I felt toward Jackson when I left Bent Creek all those years ago, need to hold on to it—for my heart's sake."

"Your heart?" he pressed.

She lifted her teary gaze. "I was in love with Jackson," she admitted to Justin for the first time ever. "But I was young and foolish, and in my girlish dreams believed that we were meant to be together. I told him as much the summer before I left for college. What I didn't take into consideration was the possibility that Jackson's heart was already taken—by the rodeo. I was and would always be nothing more than his best friend's little sister."

"Jackson told you that?" He looked shocked by her admission.

Lainie nodded. "Not in those exact words, but his feelings where I was concerned were clear enough." She swiped a hand across a tear-dampened cheek and straightened her shoulders.

"That's why you never came home to visit when rodeo season was over," Justin said knowingly. "You didn't want to risk running into Jackson."

"Yes."

"Lainie, I'll be honest," he said. "There was a time when I thought the two of you might end up together someday. And the rodeo wasn't all Jackson cared about. No matter what he told you, I know you meant a lot to him."

Not enough. "It doesn't matter," she told him. "Our lives went in the directions they were meant to. I met Will and we had Lucas. Those were two of the biggest blessings in my life. I've lost one of those blessings. I won't lose Lucas. If Jackson Wade can make a difference where my son is concerned, then I will spend every second of the day with him if need be."

"Are you certain?" Her brother studied her with a worried frown. "The last thing I'd want to do is bring about more pain for you."

She met his troubled gaze. "Jackson and I have agreed to put any issues we might have aside and focus on helping Lucas."

"Do you still love him?" he asked quietly.

Lainie didn't have to ask who. She knew he was referring to Jackson. Her immediate response, perhaps too immediate, was to shake her head in denial. "I married Will," she said. "I loved Will."

"I know you did," he said, his words low and sorrowful. "And Will loved you."

"There's someone at my window," a small, sleepy voice announced from the doorway.

Lainie looked up to find her son standing there, eyes droopy with sleep. He didn't appear frightened, making her wonder if he had dreamed the sound.

Justin stood and walked over to his nephew. "It's all right," he told him, placing a reassuring hand on Lucas's pajama-clad shoulder. "No one's out there. It's just a gnarled old tree branch tapping against the outside of your window. I haven't had time to trim it back. Every time the wind kicks up, it brushes against the windowpane."

"Maybe Mr. Wade could trim it for you," Lucas suggested with a tired smile.

"I'll see to it," Lainie said, not about to ask anything more of Jackson than she or her brother already had.

Her brother and her son looked to her in surprise at her announcement.

"I grew up on a ranch," she said, setting the book aside as she pushed to her feet. "I know how to work a handsaw." She crossed the room to where they stood in the living room entryway. "Now, let's get you back to bed." She started to reach for Lucas, but he pulled away.

"I want Uncle Justin to put me back to bed."

Her brother cast her an apologetic glance.

She gave a nod, letting him know that it was okay. This was nothing new for her, but she prayed with Jackson's help and the guidance of the Lord's gentle hand her son would eventually return to her completely. She missed tucking him in. Missed placing a loving kiss atop his head before turning out his light. Missed the sweet exchange of good-nights they used to share.

"I'm going to turn in myself," she said. "Lucas and I have a busy day planned for tomorrow."

"Mr. Wade is taking us to see his rodeo horses," her son said excitedly.

Jackson was taking them to his parents' ranch. Lucas had been asking to see the horses ever since he'd heard talk of them. Reaching out, Lainie touched her son's cheek. "Sleep well, sweetie." She wasn't surprised when he pulled away from her loving gesture, but it still hurt. Turning to her brother, she rose up on tiptoe to kiss his cheek. "I'm going to go take care of that pesky branch and then go to bed. Good night."

"Same to you," Justin replied, but Lainie knew that sleep for her that night would be a long time coming.

"Look at the deer!" Lucas exclaimed the next day as they turned onto the gravel road leading up to the main ranch house where Jackson's parents lived. A half dozen plastic reindeer sporting green wreaths around their necks, some looking off into the distance, others with their heads lowered to the ground below as if busily feasting, lined one side of the long drive.

"That's just the beginning of my mom and dad's ever-growing Christmas decor," Jackson said with a grin as he veered off the drive in the direction of the barn.

"Your parents' place looks so festive," Lainie remarked, her gaze fixed on the sight outside the passenger window. "Although I have to admit it's been a few years since I saw a grain bin decorated for the holidays. I can only imagine how pretty all this is when it's lit up at night."

Jackson smiled and gave a nod of agreement. "Mom and Dad like to go all out for Christmas, stringing garland and bows and bright, twinkling lights on anything and everything they can." And he wasn't exaggerating. Decorative garlands were draped across his parents' front porch, around the barn's windows and doors, and along the drive, draped from temporary stakes. "If they weren't afraid the horses would make a meal of the fake greenery like Tucker's horse did with Blue's favorite doll, they would no doubt have strung it along all the fencing near the house."

"Oh no," she gasped.

"It ate a doll?" Lucas chimed in from the back seat of the extended cab.

"Tried to," Jackson answered with a grin. "But we took the doll to Garrett, who stitched it back together in no time."

"I'm so glad," Lainie said with a sigh of relief and then turned to glance back at her son. "Jackson's older brother is an animal doctor, so he's naturally quite handy with a thread and needle."

"That's a big nativity set," Lucas stated as if his mother hadn't just been speaking to him.

His grin threatening to drop into a frown, Jackson fought hard not to show his dislike of Lucas's treatment of his mother. Like a mustang, the boy needed to be worked carefully, slowly gaining his trust before trying to implement changes in his behavior. "My brothers and I built the manger the nativity set is in," he said evenly. "We bring it out every Christmas and then break it down and store it away in the barn afterward."

"That sounds like a lot of work," Lainie noted as her gaze remained fixed on the festive ranch beyond her window.

"It's not bad with three of us putting it up and then taking it down," he answered. "It makes Mom happy and that's what matters." His gaze shifted to the rearview mirror just in time to see Lucas's brows pinch together, as if in silent disagreement.

They parked in front of the oversize barn and then Jackson cut the engine. "This is where we keep and care for all of our rodeo horses." He pointed off into the distance. "As usual, the herd is busy chasing each other around and expending some of their lively energy."

"Wow," Lucas exclaimed. "There are so many of them. Mom, can I go watch them from the fence?"

"If Jackson thinks that would be okay," she replied with a smile.

"As long as you stay on this side of the fence," Jackson told him. "We'll take a look at them a little closer than that some other time."

With a whoop, Lainie's son unbuckled his seat belt, threw open his door and scrambled out of the truck, racing across the yard as fast as his legs would carry him.

Jackson glanced in Lainie's direction, noting the moisture filling her eyes. He reached over, covering her hand with his own. "You okay?"

She nodded with a small sniffle. "He's coming back," she said, her words filled with emotion. "Little by little." Then she looked his way with a wavering smile. "I know things between Lucas and me are still strained, but I see him letting down his guard elsewhere. I can't even remember the last time I heard my son squeal in excitement over anything, and I have you to thank for it."

"I'm not sure I can take any of the credit for it," he told her, looking away. "Could be a lot of things pulling together to set your son at ease emotionally. I'm sure Sacramento must have painful memories following his father's death. Being away from that might be a big part of the changes you're seeing, even if he acts as if he doesn't want to be here. And another positive is his having family here to shower him with love."

"I'm sure those things all have had some impact on Lucas," she agreed. "But I still think the time you've been spending with my son has made a very positive impression on him." Her hand turned over beneath his and she curled her fingers around it, giving it a grateful squeeze. "Thank you, Jackson. I know I don't deserve your kindness. Not after the way I've treated you since that night at the Old West Festival Dance, but—"

"Don't apologize," he said, cutting her off. He looked down at their joined hands and an emotion he didn't want to feel slid through him. One he had set aside years before when Lainie married another man. An emotion he wouldn't allow to take root ever again. For her sake and for his. "I handled things badly that night. Helping you with Lucas is my way of making up for the hurt I caused you."

"Whatever the reason, I will forever be grateful," she said softly and then slowly withdrew her hand.

He cleared the sudden tightness from his throat and reached down to undo his seat belt. "I need to see to a few things in the barn. You and Lucas can wait for me at the fence or meet me at the house. I'm sure Mom's already spotted us out here and is champing at the bit to see you."

Lainie let herself out before he could come around to do so.

"I would have helped you down," he muttered not-so-happily.

"I grew up here, remember?" she said, a small smile lifting the corners of her mouth. "I know how to get in and out of a pickup truck."

"Always a country girl at heart," he noted.

"Always," she replied, and then turned, her focus returning to her son as she moved toward him.

Jackson stood watching her walk away, once again wondering what his life might have been like if he hadn't pushed Lainie away that night she'd opened up her heart to him. Would they have gotten married, had children? Would he have devoted as much time to the rodeo? Would he have been happier than what he'd come to accept as being his lot in life?

Shaking his head, he turned and headed for the barn, deciding that some questions were better off left unanswered.

Lainie moved to stand beside her son, but her attention wasn't centered on the horses that seemed to fascinate him so. It was on Jackson's departing form. Being a country girl wasn't the only thing that seemed to be permanently imbedded in her heart. She curled her fingers reflexively inside her coat pocket, the ones she'd threaded through Jackson's only moments before as she felt that old tug of yearning she'd worked so hard to get over. The want of sharing the easygoing friendship they had once shared. A friendship she had ruined by wanting something that was never meant to be. She'd reacted poorly to his rejection when she should have appreciated his honesty. But at that moment in her young life his words felt devastating, life changing in a way she wasn't prepared for, and she'd reacted by shutting him out of her life.

Closing her eyes, Lainie sent up a silent prayer. *Lord, please help me to mend the fences that I have broken where Jackson Wade is concerned.* Because she truly had missed having him in her life.

Another vehicle rolled up the drive, drawing Lainie's attention that way. A second later, she recognized Tucker behind the wheel of the approaching pickup. *These Wade brothers and their need for big trucks*, she thought with a grin. Then again, they were ranchers. Big trucks were pretty much a necessity.

The vehicle rolled to a stop next to Jackson's and Tucker got out, offering a nod of greeting as he strode in her and her son's direction. "Lainie," he greeted.

"Hello, Tucker," Lainie said with an anxious smile, unsure of how Jackson's brother would feel about her being there after all the distance she had put between herself and Jackson all those years.

No animosity touched his countenance, only a warm grin as his gaze came to rest on her son.

"No Autumn?" Jackson inquired.

His brother shook his head. "She and Hannah are coming together. They should be here shortly." His gaze shifted to Lainie's son. "Who do we have here?"

Lainie wrapped an arm around Lucas's small shoulders. "Tucker, this is my son, Lucas."

"You look like Mr. Wade," her son remarked as he stood staring up at the youngest of the Wade brothers.

"That's because I am Mr. Wade," Tucker replied with a widening grin. Then he held out a hand. "I'm Tucker Wade. Jackson's younger brother."

Lucas eyed the offered hand and then reached out to take hold. "Are you the one who takes care of sick animals and fixes broken dolls?"

"Jackson told you about that, did he?" he said with a glance up at Lainie.

"He mentioned it," she answered.

Looking down once more at Lucas, he said, "Our older brother, Garrett, is the animal doctor. And doll doctor, I suppose, and thankfully so. It nearly broke my little girl's heart when my horse tried to eat her doll baby. Jackson came up with the idea of using a mop to replace the hair Blue's doll lost in the tussle, so I guess you can say both of my brothers came to the rescue. Thanks to them, Molly is all in one piece and has stayed far away from the pasture fences ever since."

"Would they eat my hair?" her son asked, sounding more curious than fearful.

Tucker chuckled. "I think you're safe."

His gaze lifting to Lainie, he said, "No one told me we were having company join us for dinner."

"That's because I haven't asked them yet."

Lainie turned to see Jackson moving toward them. "We're having a family dinner tonight. And since Justin will be working, I was hoping you and Lucas might agree to join us."

She shook her head. "Oh, we couldn't impose on you like that."

"Then we'll call it a family and friends dinner," Tucker said. "Autumn has been champing at the bit to meet you."

Jackson nodded. "So has Hannah, according to Garrett."

"They are?" she asked in surprise.

Jackson chuckled in response. "They are. Probably because Mom has been talking you up since she found out you had come home. Garrett and Dad won't be here, however," he told her. "They and the crew took horses to Vegas for the NFR. Tucker stayed home to look after the ranch and his and Autumn's newest addition to the family."

"And Jackson stayed home to look after you and Lucas," Tucker added with a grin.

Lainie stiffened, guilt wrapping around her so thickly it was hard to breathe. Not only had she been the cause of Jackson putting off his own personal business interests, the NFR was the rodeo Jackson had been competing in that day she'd called to tell him she was getting married. The night he'd nearly died.

"What's NFR?" her son asked curiously.

"Just another rodeo," she forced out, praying her son wouldn't ask any more about it.

"Not just another rodeo," Tucker announced. "It's the premier championship event in the United States. The best of the best compete there for the world title."

Lainie's gaze shifted to Jackson. Unable to help herself, she let her gaze drop down to the leg he'd injured while competing for one of those world titles.

"Jackson is the only one of us to make it to the finals," Tucker went on.

"Did he win?" her son asked in awe.

Lainie looked up to find Jackson watching her, his expression unreadable.

"No," he said evenly, "I didn't."

She looked away, focusing on nothing in particular.

"He came close to winning," Tucker said in his brother's defense. "Should have. He was the best of the lot. But the bull he drew that evening was one of the meanest, most stubborn pieces of bovine flesh ever to enter the arena."

"Tucker," she heard Jackson say, "why don't you take Lucas over and show him the double-decker?"

"What's a double-decker?" Lucas asked, excitement filling his voice.

"It's one of the trailers we use to transport horses to the rodeos during the rodeo season," Tucker replied. "They call it that because you can put horses up on the top level as well as the bottom." He looked to Lainie. "Mind if I give him a short ride in it?"

"A ride?" she repeated anxiously.

"A short one," he assured her. "I need to pull it away from the barn and over to the hose across the way." He pointed to a faucet that stood alone about thirty feet or so away from the grain bin Lainie had seen when they pulled in. "While the other trailer is gone, I'll look this one over and then give it a good cleaning."

"Can I, Mom?" her son pleaded.

"If you're not comfortable with it..." Jackson began.

Lainie shook her head. "No, it's all right. It's not like they're going far."

Tucker gave a nod of acknowledgment, clearly understanding her reservations. Even if they went beyond the front area of the ranch, she knew Lucas would be safe with Tucker. With all of the Wades. Men she had grown up around and still trusted.

Her son gave a loud whoop. "Can I help you clean it?" he asked as he followed Tucker away, attempting to mimic his long, cowboy strides.

Lainie turned her gaze back to the horses roaming about across the rolling hills, still shaken by Tucker's mention of the Vegas rodeo and how close Jackson had come to taking the title home. A title she knew he had deserved, because she had still followed his career from afar.

"Lainie..." Jackson said behind her.

She should have insisted on joining Lucas on the tour, because she couldn't bear to face Jackson right at that moment.

"I'm so sorry about Vegas," she forced out, the words catching as emotion flooded her.

"It wasn't your fault."

She squeezed her eyes shut. "Yes," she said, the word almost a whisper, "it was."

"You heard Tucker," he said, a hint of tenderness in his voice. "The bull I drew that night was the best of the lot."

She swung her teary-eyed gaze around to meet his. "I never should have called you that day. If I hadn't…" She let the thought trail off.

"Why did you call me, Lainie?" he asked, searching her face.

She let out a sob. "To hurt you. Only I hurt you more than I ever dreamed possible." She tipped her head into his hand, a tear sliding down her face. "I'm so sorry, Jackson."

He reached up to cup her cheek. "There's nothing to forgive. It was man against beast. The beast just happened to be better that day."

"Jackson, you nearly died, and whether you are willing to admit it or not I know in my heart that my call had something to do with your fall. And then I hurt my husband as well. Only Will died because I acted on my emotions," she sobbed.

The next thing she knew, she was in Jackson's comforting arms, her head resting against his broad shoulder. "Will's death wasn't your fault."

All the grief she'd been holding in was released in that moment. "I was driving that night," she admitted. "I should've seen that boy running the red light. Should have reacted faster. But I didn't, and his car struck the passenger side head-on. Will's side."

"Lainie." He sighed into her hair as he comforted her. "I had no idea what really happened that night, only that your car was struck by a drunk driver. But this changes nothing. You aren't to blame for what happened that night. You weren't the one who drank far too much and then slid behind the wheel of a car. That boy was."

"I keep thinking that if I had taken a different way home," she said, "or if we had stayed later at Will's company party…"

"It was Will's time to go," he said softly. "You couldn't have changed that."

Hot tears slid down her cheeks.

"Lainie, we both know that sometimes things happen in our life that we have no control over, things we don't understand. Like Will's dying, my sister's dying, even the fall that ended my rodeo career. At least, the riding side of it," he added. "We just have to stay strong in our faith and continue on. The Lord will guide us through the tough times."

She lifted her head to look up at him. "I'm trying my best to carry on, but it's so hard. My son is shutting me out. I no longer have a place to call my own. And I have to rely on others to get around, because I can't bring myself to get behind the wheel of a car again."

Leaning back, he cupped her chin and tipped her face up to his. "Lucas is getting better every day. You've said so yourself. And we'll find you a place of your own. Autumn can help. She knows every listing in the area." He searched her tear-streaked face. "And you will drive again. I'll do whatever it takes to help you make that happen. I promise."

She looked up into his handsome face with a soft sniffle. "Jackson," she said in a choked whisper, touched so very much by his kindness.

The tractor trailer on the other side of the barn revved to life, drawing Lainie's gaze that way. Realizing that it would be pulling out any moment, she took a step back from Jackson, whose hand fell away. She couldn't allow her son to see her being comforted. Not when it was her job as his mother to be strong.

A second later, Tucker eased the truck out from where it had been parked, next to the barn, driving in a slow, wide arc around the yard, finally coming to a stop beside the place where several water pipes rose up from the ground.

Turning away, she hurried to dry her eyes.

"Stay for dinner," Jackson said as he moved to stand next to her. "Talk to Autumn about finding a place. Take in the slightly overdone Christmas light display Mom is so proud of."

He managed to get a small smile from her. Drying her eyes, she said, "You can never have too many Christmas lights."

"Lainie!"

Their gazes swung around in the direction of the front porch, where Jackson's mother stood drying her hands on what looked to be a kitchen towel.

"Mrs. Wade," Lainie replied with forced cheeriness.

The other woman draped the towel she was holding over the railing and then stepped down from the porch. "Call me Emma," she gently scolded as she crossed the yard to where they stood at the fence. "I tell you that every time you come home to visit." Leaning in, she gave Lainie a warm, welcoming hug.

"It's hard not to call you Mrs. Wade," she admitted. "That's all I ever called you growing up."

"Well, you're not a little girl anymore," his mother

replied with a smile. "You're a grown woman. Speaking of which," she said, her gaze meeting Jackson's for only a moment before looking past them, "where is that handsome little boy of yours?"

"He's over helping Tucker with the trailer," Lainie said.

Emma's gaze drifted past her. "I hope Tucker doesn't get too caught up in what he's doing. Dinner will be ready soon." Looking back to Lainie, she said, "You will be joining us this evening, won't you? I'm anxious for my girls to meet you."

Her girls. It was so endearing to hear Emma speak of her daughters-in-law that way. Lainie had once dreamed she might someday become one, a true part of the Wade family. "I wouldn't want to intrude."

Emma let out a guffaw. "Honey, you spent so much time around my family growing up, you're practically one of us. Please stay for dinner. I know Autumn and Hannah would love to have a chance to get to know you and that sweet little boy of yours."

Lainie smiled. "Then we'll stay."

"They're here," Jackson's mother exclaimed as she sprang up from the chair by the living room window. Jackson chuckled, murmuring with a grin, "One would never guess by your reaction that Autumn and Hannah are here all the time."

"Yes, but now I have another new grandbaby to fuss over," she replied with another glance out the front window. "And this will be the first time they get to meet Lainie and Lucas."

He glanced over to where Lainie sat in the rocking chair his mother bought the moment Garrett and

Hannah had announced their engagement. She had said that a grandmother—referring to what she would officially be to Hannah's newborn son when they married—needed a rocker to rock her grandbaby, and any future grandbabies. Jackson found himself envisioning Lainie with an infant resting trustingly in her arms as she lulled the child to sleep. *His* child. And then he tore his gaze away. The last thing he needed to be doing was imagining a future he would never have, because he never intended to marry. He couldn't bear the thought of his wife, whoever she might be, seeing his damaged leg, scars and all, her eyes filling with pity. Watching him limp around while other men moved about with confident, unhindered strides. Or just simply looking at his leg, emotions unreadable, as Lainie had done earlier.

Jackson stood. "I'll go out and help them in. Lord knows they travel with a lot of stuff nowadays, between baby carriers, diaper bags and really big purses filled with whatever it is you ladies like to carry around with you."

"No," his mother said. "You stay and keep Lainie and Lucas company. I'll go help with the babies." Without waiting for his response, his mother hurried from the room.

Jackson looked to Lainie with a shrug.

Smiling, she said, "It's what grandmas do. Mom was the same way when I had Lucas."

The pitter-patter of tiny feet preceded the entrance of his niece as Blue raced into the living room. "Uncle Jackson!"

Opening his arms, he caught her as she jumped up into them. "My favorite girl," he said with a grin as he

"Are you Uncle Jackson's friend? Momma said she'd be here."

She looked his way as if unsure how to answer Blue's question.

"She is," Jackson answered for her. She would always be his friend, even when she wished otherwise. "Ms. Dawson," Jackson said, wanting his niece to be respectful when referring to Lainie, "is an old family friend."

"Michaels," she promptly corrected him.

Jackson fought a frown at the error he had made. It hadn't been intentional. Or had it? Because there was a part of his mind that had always refused to accept the truth. That Lainie had chosen to love another. "Ms. Michaels," he acknowledged with a nod.

Blue studied Lainie for a long moment before saying, "She doesn't look old."

The corners of Jackson's mouth twitched when Lainie's gaze met his. "She's not. That just means we've been friends for a very long time. Since we were even younger than you." He returned his attention to Blue. "You remember Sheriff Dawson."

She nodded.

"He's Ms. Michaels's brother."

She looked to Lainie. "Are you a sheriff, too?"

She shook her head. "No. I'm a… Well, I used to be an accountant. Then I had my son, Lucas, and became a full-time mother."

"Is he a baby?"

"No, he's seven," she replied. "He'll be eight in a little over a week."

Jackson looked to her in surprise. "He will? I didn't realize he had a birthday coming up."

lifted her with ease. His niece brought such sunshine into their lives, giving his mother such immense joy, and turning the rough and tough hearts of each and every Wade male to butter. She was also a reminder. If he had accepted Lainie's love back then, they might have had a family of their own to share meals with and spend holidays together. He supposed that someday he might have those things, but there had never been anyone since Lainie to stir those longing in him. He wasn't sure there ever would be.

The moment Blue's gaze landed on Lainie, her smile widened. "Hello."

"Hello to you, too," Lanie replied as she stood to greet her. "You must be Blue."

His niece nodded. "I am. My baby brother, T.J., is out there with Momma Autumn." The sound of women's laughter and happy chatter confirmed their whereabouts. "She's my aunt, but Daddy said she's allowed to be my momma, too, if I want her to be, 'cause my momma is in Heaven."

"You are a very blessed little girl to have two mommies watching over you," Lainie said as she crossed the room to stand with them. "One here on Earth and the other from Heaven above."

Blue seemed to consider that for a moment and then smiled. "I am. What's your name?"

"Lainie," she replied.

"That's a pretty name," his niece said.

For a pretty girl, Jackson mentally agreed. No, Lainie wasn't a girl any longer. She was a woman now. As beautiful as she was smart.

Lainie's smile softened. "So is Blue."

"He does," she said with a soft sigh. "If only we could keep our children babies forever."

"Then we would never have any fun," Blue said with a slight frown. "All we would be able to do is lay around while everyone talks funny and makes silly faces at us. And eat yucky baby food," she added, screwing up her face at the thought of it.

His niece's reply had Lainie laughing. "You have a point," she conceded. She leaned toward Blue in a conspiratorial whisper, "Babies don't lead very exciting lives. Not like little boys and girls your age do."

"Did Uncle Jackson bring you here?" she asked.

"I did," Jackson answered.

His niece looked up at him from her perch in his arms. "Does that mean you're gonna marry her? 'Cause Uncle Garrett brought Aunt Hannah to Grandma's and he married her."

His response was choked. "No. Lainie and I are not getting married." Much to his everlasting regret.

Blue's face registered disappointment. Thankfully, before she could pursue the matter any further his mother, sisters-in-law and their little ones entered the room.

Jackson set Blue on her feet and then moved to stand beside Lainie. "These pretty ladies are my sisters-in-law. The one holding the empty baby carrier Mom wasted no time in confiscating my new nephew from is Tucker's wife, Autumn."

His mother beamed with joy as she stood, cooing over her newest grandchild.

"And the one preparing to have her baby removed from her arms by my mother next is Hannah, Garrett's wife, which is why I'm going to snag him first."

"He's all yours," Hannah said, laughing softly.

As he settled his oldest nephew, baby Austin, into the crook of his arm, he felt the usual tug of yearning at his heart that he felt whenever he held one of his brothers' children. He hoped his siblings realized just how lucky they were.

"Look at him," his mother said with a grin, "so caught up in my grandbaby that he forgot what it was he was in the middle of doing."

Jackson's head snapped up and a tinge of warmth moved through his cheeks. "Sorry," he said. "Autumn, Hannah, I'd like you to meet Lainie Michaels. She's Justin's little sister."

"It's a pleasure to finally meet you."

They smiled warmly at Lainie.

"It's so nice to finally meet you, too," Hannah said.

Autumn nodded. "Emma has done nothing but chatter on about you since she found out you had moved back to Bent Creek. Not that we mind," she hurried to add. "It's clear how much they care about you and your brother."

"We were all very close growing up," she said, her gaze lifting to meet Jackson's.

His mother must have noticed her discomfort, because she added, "Justin and Jackson were like brothers, blood related or not, and Lainie was like a daughter to me."

"You were like a second mother to me," Lainie replied, her eyes misting over.

His mother smiled warmly as she swayed back and forth, cradling her newborn grandson in her arms. "It's so good to have you home." Her gaze shifted to Jackson. "Honey, why don't you run out and get your brother and Lucas? Tell them to come in and wash up while I put dinner on the table before it gets cold."

With a nod, Jackson handed his eight-month-old nephew back to Hannah. His brother had wasted no time in setting legalities into motion to adopt Hannah's son after they wed that past September. But in Garrett's mind Austin Sanders was already his. Austin's parents, Hannah's sister and her husband, had died in an automobile accident. Hannah, also their surrogate mother, was left to raise the baby she had so selflessly carried for them. "He's growing like a weed," he told her.

She laughed. "He sure is."

"Here," Autumn said, reaching to take her son back from Emma, "let me take him. I'll settle T.J. in his carrier and then give you a hand with setting dinner out."

"May I hold him?"

Everyone's gaze shifted to Lainie.

"I mean I would be more than happy to help set the table or whatever you might need me to do." Her eyes were fixed on the sleepy infant now resting peacefully in his sister-in-law's arms. "Even hold this precious little bundle." She looked to Hannah. "Or yours. I just miss holding a little one in my arms."

Jackson watched her thoughtfully. Having lost her husband, Lainie wouldn't have the chance to do that again anytime soon. If only things had turned out differently, Jackson would have given her all the babies she cared to hold. But they hadn't, and she had been blessed with Lucas because of it. So he needed to stop allowing the if-onlys and the what-ifs to burrow into his thoughts. What mattered now was repairing his fractured friendship with Lainie, something he intended to do everything in his power to make happen. The good Lord willing, with perseverance and patience, Jackson would win Lainie's trust back.

Chapter Five

The next day, Jackson couldn't get his mind off dinner the night before. Lainie had fit in so well, making fast friends of both his sisters-in-law. Even Lucas had found a friend in Blue, who wasn't much younger than him. It was good to see Lainie's son interact so easily with Blue. Unlike the way he tended to treat Lainie, the boy was patient with his niece's never-ending questions and laughed along with her at things even Jackson couldn't figure out the humor in.

He'd not missed Lainie watching them with a look of longing that he understood. She wanted her son to be the same way with her. He had offered to give Lucas riding lessons while Autumn took Lainie around to look at houses. He wanted to have another man-to-man, or in their case, man-to-boy, with Lucas, something he had done in small doses since Lainie had agreed to allow him to assist her. He just prayed he would be able to help.

"Can I ride a really big horse?"

He looked to Lucas, who was all smiles that morning and couldn't help but think about the differences between him and Blue. At least, the way Blue had been when she first came to Bent Creek. His niece hadn't wanted anything to do with horses. But she had her reasons and had, with Tucker's gentle coaxing, worked through her fears. "Someday," he told him with a smile. "But for now we need to start with a more size-appropriate mount for you. I think Tumbleweed would be the perfect training horse for you."

"Tumbleweed?"

"He belongs to Tucker," Jackson told him. "My brother bought him for Autumn. He's a Palomino, which means he has a gold coat and white tail and mane. Used to belong to one of Tucker's old rodeo buddies, who used him for roping competitions. He's a little older, but well broke and good-natured."

"He's a rodeo horse?" Lucas repeated excitedly.

Jackson nodded. "He's seen his fair share of competitions." He reached for the barn door and drew it open. "You'll learn to ride in here to start with."

"In the arena?" he asked, having seen the small indoor training area when Jackson had first given him a tour of the main barn on his parents' property.

"Best place to get your feet wet." The expression on Lucas's face reminded Jackson of Blue's right before she questioned something that had been said. It was hard to remember kids tended to take things literally. "That means getting started on something new," he explained as he closed the barn door behind them.

"I know that," Lucas replied with an eye roll. "I'm not a baby."

Jackson chuckled. "No, Lucas, you're not."

They made their way into the barn, where Jackson

introduced Lucas to Tumbleweed and then showed him the proper way to saddle a horse.

"Can I ride now?" Lucas asked with obvious impatience.

"One more thing," Jackson told him and then walked over to grab Blue's safety helmet from its hook on the wall. "You need to wear this." He settled the protective headwear atop Lucas's head and then moved to secure the chin strap.

Lucas scrunched his face. "But it's pink."

"So is bubblegum and cotton candy–flavored yogurt and you probably like both of them." His words gave Lainie's son a moment's thought, so he added, "We'll get you another helmet to use when you come over to ride, but for now it's this one or I can't let you up on that horse. Safety is key." Not to mention he would never forgive himself if something bad happened to Lainie's son when he was in Jackson's care.

Lucas debated for only a moment before replying, "I can't ride without it?"

"Nope." It wasn't up for debate.

"But you and your brothers ride your horses without helmets…" Lucas pressed.

"We're grown men with a lot of years' experience riding horses. You've never even sat in a saddle. Big difference."

Lainie's son glanced toward the awaiting horse and then lifted his chin with the same determined tilt he'd seen Lainie do so many times. "Fine."

Jackson secured the horse's reins to a railing while he went to get the wooden mounting block Tucker had built for Blue. He placed it next to Tumbleweed and instructed Lucas on how to get himself up into the saddle.

Lucas managed to seat himself first try.

"A natural," Jackson acknowledged with a nod. "Just like your mom."

The boy's expression tightened. "I'm not like her," he countered. "I'm like my dad."

Jackson reached down to set the block aside and then unwound the reins from the wooden rail. "I'm sure you are," he said as he led the horse away from the indoor arena's fence. "But you have a lot of your mother in you. I know because I've known her all my life. I see a lot of her in you. In your determination. In your smile. And, I have a feeling, in your horseman-ship. Now let's see what you can do."

Lucas listened to Jackson's instruction as he led the horse around the dirt-packed floor of the riding arena.

Like he'd said, the boy was a natural. "Once I'm certain you're comfortable in the saddle, I'll put Tum-bleweed on a lead rope and let you take a little more control of the ride."

"Today?" he said excitedly.

Jackson shook his head. "Not today. A few more lessons first."

Surprisingly, Lucas didn't put up any argument. He just remained focused in the saddle, taking in every-thing Jackson had to tell him. They made countless laps around the arena before Jackson announced that they were done for the day.

"Can we do this again tomorrow?"

"I think your grandma and grandpa are coming to visit you and your mom tomorrow," Jackson reminded him as he led the horse over to the arena gate.

"And you," Lucas prompted with a boyish smile.

"I won't be there," Jackson told him. Lainie had

informed him of her parents' impending visit, telling him there was no need for him to come by to check on them. He intended to respect her wishes where her family was concerned, as much as he enjoyed spending time with her and Lucas. "I have ranch duties to see to tomorrow." He secured the horse and then placed the mounting steps next to it. "Now hold on to that saddle horn and swing your right leg slowly over Tumbleweed's backside. Then ease down the left side until you feel the block under your boot."

Lucas followed his instructions to a tee.

"That's it," Jackson praised with a nod. "Now slip your other foot free of the stirrup and then step down slowly."

"How's come we have to do everything slow?"

"Tumbleweed's a pretty easygoing horse, but a sudden movement, especially from a rider he's not familiar with, could cause him to sidestep unexpectedly and knock you over. Even throw a rider if he or she was still in the saddle," he explained.

"Is that how you hurt your leg?"

The boy's question took Jackson aback for a brief moment. Most people tended to avoid pointing out his physical disability. Although, as he'd learned with Blue, children tended to speak their mind, despite the discomfort their doing so sometimes caused others. His lips pressed together at the reminder of his ever-present limp. Sometimes he forgot he even had one, having lived with it for so many years. Only the onset of bad weather, which made his leg ache, drew his focus to it. Well, that and Lainie's return. Her being back, spending time with him, made Jackson wonder what she thought about whenever she saw his uneven gait. While she'd done her best to hide it, he'd caught her on more than one occasion studying his jean-clad leg. Her expression was not one of pity, but something Jackson hadn't been able to read.

Reaching for the portable steps, he set them aside and then unwound Tumbleweed's reins. "It happened from a fall, but not from a horse," he said as he led the horse out of the arena and back to its stall, Lucas walking alongside him. He signaled for Lucas to wait outside the stall as he led Tumbleweed inside. "I was thrown from a bull during a rodeo and managed to end up under its hooves," he explained as he stepped around the horse's neck to remove its saddle.

"Bulls are big," Lucas exclaimed as he watched from the stall's entrance. "I've seen them on TV when Mom watches rodeos."

Jackson's head snapped up, his gaze zeroing in on Lainie's son. "Your mom watches rodeos?"

"Only when your horses are at them," he clarified with a toothy grin. "She says the Triple W has the best rodeo stock around. But I think she likes the part afterward when they talk to people who are a part of the rodeo. We saw you on there once and she got so excited."

"She did?"

Lucas nodded. "And then she got kind of quiet. Like she was sad. Maybe because she didn't want the rodeo to be over. She doesn't watch anything else."

Lainie followed the televised rodeos? No, only the rodeos at which the Triple W had stock. "It's possible," Jackson muttered, his thoughts on what Lucas had just told him. He had a feeling that seeing him on television had been the reason for her mood change, no doubt reminding her of the heartache he'd caused her. It ate at him that his actions so many years before had affected Lainie so deeply when all he'd wanted was the best for her.

"Riding lesson over?"

They both turned to see Tucker striding toward the stall. "For today," Jackson answered as he lifted the saddle from Tumbleweed's back.

"Sorry I missed seeing this young cowboy in the saddle," his brother said, looking to Lucas. "How'd it go?"

"He's a natural," Jackson said, smiling as Lainie's son drew back his shoulders and lifted his chin.

"It was fun," Lucas said.

"Glad you enjoyed yourself," Tucker told him and then looked to Jackson. "I just got off the phone with Kade. He's good to go for the Wilmont Rodeo. He said for us to shoot him over the contract and he'll sign on."

Jackson nodded. "I'll do that this evening after I get back from taking Lucas and Lainie home."

"Sounds good. I'll let you two finish up here," Tucker said. "Mom wants me to take a look at the chicken coop door. It blew shut on her the other day and latched, locking her inside. Thankfully, Dad was sitting on the front porch drinking a cup of coffee. Otherwise, she might have been in there for a good while."

"No kidding," Jackson agreed, considering he'd been spending a great deal of time over at Justin's place. "Let me know if you need a hand."

"I will."

"Who's Kade?" Lucas asked when Tucker had gone.

"He's our business partner. He lives in Oklahoma

on a cattle ranch where he raises bulls for the rodeo. We contract together. We bring the rodeo horses and he brings the bulls." They were supposed to be talking about Lucas's relationship with Lainie, not about him. How had they gotten so sidetracked? Jackson stepped from the stall, closing the gate behind him.

"Were you ever scared of getting up on a bull?"

"Every time I climbed onto one," Jackson admitted. "A rodeo cowboy would be in the wrong profession if he weren't a little afraid. And that's nothing to be ashamed of. Fear just means you have a healthy respect for what the animal is capable of."

"Maybe I'll ride bulls when I grow up."

Lord, he hoped not. If anything happened to Lucas, Lainie would never forgive him, even if he'd done nothing to encourage him. Truth was, he never would. Lucas was too precious to Lainie and Jackson knew firsthand what could happen with one bad ride. He lived with the reminder of it every day of his life.

"There are a lot of things you can become," Jackson told him. "I wouldn't set your mind on anything yet. You might find you'll want to be something else when you grow up. Like a doctor, or a teacher, maybe even a clown in a circus."

Lucas burst into laughter. "A clown?"

Jackson grinned and reach out to playfully pinch the tip of Lucas's nose. "One with a big red honker."

The boy giggled and shook his head, then lifted his gaze to Jackson's face. "I think I'd rather grow up to be a cowboy just like you."

Warmth spread through Jackson's heart. "Maybe you will, kiddo. Maybe you will."

* * *

"Well," Autumn said with a smile as she settled in behind the wheel of her car, "what did you really think about this place?"

Lainie glanced out the window toward the house she and Autumn had just walked through. "It's nice."

"So you told the listing Realtor who was holding this open house. I'm not so sure I buy that. Not when you've said the same thing about the other two houses we saw this morning."

She looked to Autumn, unsure of what to say. "I'm sorry to keep you away from your little one when I don't seem to be in the house-buying mood today."

"First of all, as much as I love being a mother, it's nice to have a little time away," Autumn told her. "And Emma is more than happy to watch her grandson while I'm out showing you houses. Blue, on the other hand, is practically attached to her daddy's hip. You can pretty much bet she went over to her grandparents' place today with the intention of shadowing her daddy everywhere he goes. So there's no hurry." She smiled reflectively, before adding, "To be honest, it feels good to get back into the swing of things again. I hired on a couple of part-time real estate agents when I neared the end of my pregnancy, so I could focus on my family and bringing my son safely into the world. And while I don't intend to go back to work full-time, I have been itching to get back at it. So thank you for giving me a reason to do so."

"You're welcome," Lainie said with a smile. "I was beginning to feel like I was wasting your time this afternoon."

"Lainie," Autumn said, shifting slightly in the driver's

seat to face her, "you do realize that you don't have to like every house I show you. You don't even have to pretend to. If it's not for you, it's not for you. I wanna find what *you* want. Not settle for anything less. But you need to be honest about what you do and don't like. Otherwise, I'll keep showing you places that are just 'nice.'"

As for finding what she wanted, she had wanted Jackson. That hadn't turned out so well. And while she honestly didn't feel as though she had settled for less in marrying Will—if anything she had been blessed to have him in her life—it hadn't been the life she had once envisioned for her future. Just as the houses they had seen hadn't been her idea of the sort of homes she pictured herself raising Lucas in. But her marriage had also taught her not to look past something that might be a good fit for her because she was searching for something else. However, this particular house was not the one. Neither were the two others. She felt that in her heart.

"Honesty, huh?" she repeated.

"I'm from Texas," Autumn said with a grin, as if her deep Southern twang hadn't already given her away. "I promise you I can take it."

Lainie laughed softly. "Okay. The houses we've seen so far have all been very nice. But they're not what I envisioned Lucas and I living in when we decided to move back here. They're all so—" she searched for the right word, finally settling for "—contemporary?"

"That's good to know," Jackson's sister-in-law said with a nod. "I just figured you were used to a more modernized home, having moved back from such a large city and all."

"The condo we had in California was definitely modern, but I'm a country girl at heart," Lainie confessed.

"Country girl," Autumn repeated as she withdrew a notepad from her purse and jotted it down. Then she glanced up at Lainie. "Go on. Because something tells me there's more you're actually looking for than the three-bedroom, two-bath, single-level house with a yard that you specified."

"I prefer a house that's close to town. One with a large porch that stretches across the front of it, maybe even wraps around it, where I'd be able to sit out in the evening and watch the sun settle behind the mountains, dappling everything around it in spectacular shades of red and gold. I've always wanted a cedar-sided house, but it's not a deal-killer if it's not. I would like there to be a barn we could keep two or three horses in."

That caught Autumn's attention. "You ride?"

"I used to. Although it's been a while," she admitted. "I'm sure you already know that my brother and Jackson were best friends growing up, still are actually, and we grew up on ranches that bordered each other."

Autumn nodded her reply.

"We were always out riding together when we were younger. Although I was only with them because Mom told Justin he couldn't go without me. That's how I got so good at riding. They would try to race off without me. But I was lighter, and my horse, much to their chagrin, was faster, and I would end up passing them both." She couldn't help but smile at the fond memory.

Autumn laughed. "Typical boys. And good for you for showing them what you were made of."

She'd always loved riding, but she'd only learned

to do it as well as she did to make Jackson take notice of her, which he had, always praising her riding skills. "Justin doesn't ride much anymore," she said, changing the subject. "He spends most of his time inside his patrol car or in his office, working."

"Sounds like Hannah's friend Jessica. She's a neonatal nurse at the local hospital who takes on extra shifts to support herself and her son, Dustin."

"I take it she's a single mother."

"Yes."

"Who watches her son while she's at work?" That was something Lainie had been blessed not to have to worry about. She hadn't worked since before having Lucas and hadn't needed to since Will's passing. Her husband had left them financially secure, but then that was the kind of man he was. Always thinking ahead, putting his family's needs before his own.

"She had been living with her mother, who would look after Jessica's son when she worked, but she passed away unexpectedly a few months ago."

"Oh no. I'm sorry to hear that."

"Hannah's been watching Dustin for her, which has been a blessing for Jessica, but she lives near the hospital, so bringing her son to Bent Creek is more than a little out of the way. That's why she's considering moving here. She'd only have the drive to the hospital instead of from the city to Bent Creek and then back to the city again. In fact, I'm going to be showing her a few places around town tomorrow."

"Well, we've certainly seen some—"

"Nice ones?" Autumn said, cutting her off with a teasing smile.

Lainie laughed. "Exactly." She liked Tucker's wife

a whole lot. Garrett's, too. Only she hadn't gotten to spend as much time with Hannah, but she hoped they would have the opportunity to get to know each other a lot better in the near future.

"Getting back to the house hunt," Autumn prompted. "I want to know what you see when you imagine the place you want to settle down in with your son."

Lainie thought for a moment. "I've always wanted a place with a large picture window in the front of the house. One I can display our Christmas tree in when the holiday rolls around each year. And a fireplace, or maybe a woodstove, would help make a house feel cozy. Lots of cupboards and maybe a farm-style sink in the kitchen." She looked to Autumn. "Too much to ask for?"

"Not at all. This helps a great deal. In fact, it tells me that I should sweet-talk Jackson into selling you his place. It fits your list perfectly."

Lainie's eyes widened. *It did?* While she had spent a lot of time at the main ranch house growing up, she'd never been inside Jackson or his brothers' homes, which had been built after she had gone away to college. All she really knew about Jackson's place was that he had a wraparound porch with the oversize window she hoped to have in whatever home she decided on buying. "I don't think any amount of sweet-talking is going to convince your brother-in-law to sell his place."

"Probably not," Autumn agreed. "But I'm sure I can find something that would fit most of your requirements." She glanced in the direction of the home they'd just toured. "We should probably get going or the listing Realtor is going to think we're out here writing up an offer."

"I should be getting back to the ranch anyhow," Lainie said with a sigh. "Jackson will probably be wondering where we are." He'd been kind enough to offer to watch Lucas for her while she went house-hunting. He'd even offered to teach her son how to saddle and ride a horse. If it had been anyone else, she might have had reservations about him doing so without her there. But she trusted Jackson.

That thought had her taking a mental step back. *She trusted Jackson.* Even though he'd broken her heart, she knew her son was in good hands. As if he knew she'd been thinking about him, Lainie's cell rang, the screen displaying Jackson's name and number. "Someone's ears were burning," she said, laughing softly as she answered the call. "Autumn and I were just getting ready to head back," she told him.

"I'm glad."

Why did he sound unusually tense? Like he was upset but trying to sound calm. "Jackson?" she said, sensing something was wrong. "Is everything okay?" His hesitation in responding sent a surge of panic through Lainie. Her heart began to pound in her chest. "Please tell me Lucas didn't fall off the horse," she begged, her eyes welling up with tears. "Please, Jackson."

"He didn't fall off the horse," he quickly assured her. "That boy's got his mother's genes when it comes to riding. However, he did fall."

She closed her eyes, wishing his words away. "What happened? How bad is it?" Autumn's hand came to rest atop her own in a comforting manner.

"Just a small incident at the chicken coop," he explained. "But he's doing okay."

Okay? Okay wasn't the same as *fine*. At least, not in her book. She looked to Autumn with an anxious smile as she fought to hold it together.

"Lainie? You still there?"

"Yes," she said, the word a forced whisper. "Did Lucas hit his head when he fell?"

"No. His head is fine."

Fine was better than *okay*, Lainie thought with a bit of relief. "Jackson, what happened?"

"Tucker was replacing the latch on the chicken coop door. Afterward, he planned to collect whatever eggs had been laid and save Mom a trip out there. Lucas saw the egg basket sitting off to the side and offered to go in and collect them while Tucker finished up on the door."

"But he's never collected eggs before," Lainie said.

"I know, but he wanted to do it," Jackson told her. "So we instructed him on what he needed to do and off he went. When he was done, he came out of the hen-house beaming from ear to ear. A young man proud of his accomplishment. Only he tripped on his way back down the plank and took a tumble."

"Is he okay?"

Autumn motioned that she was going to start driving.

Nodding, Lainie buckled her seat belt.

"A banged-up knee, scraped-up palms and a slightly wounded pride."

She knew Jackson was trying to make light of things to keep her from having a panic attack over her son's fall. "We're on our way." She hung up without saying goodbye, concern making it almost impossible to concentrate.

"Lainie?" Autumn said worriedly. "What's going on?"

Lainie filled her in. "I need to call Justin. He should be able to get to the ranch pretty quickly." She and Autumn were out in the country on the opposite side of town.

"If Jackson says Lucas is all right, I'm sure he is," Autumn said, her tone consoling as Lainie made the call to her brother.

She prayed Autumn was right. But a part of her feared Jackson might be holding back because of what he knew she'd already gone through with Will.

When Lainie and Autumn arrived at Tucker's parents' ranch, Justin's patrol car was already parked just outside the main house, alongside Jackson's and Tucker's trucks, and a car Lainie didn't recognize. She let herself out of Autumn's bright yellow Mustang GT and raced toward the porch.

"Lucas?" Lainie called out as she stepped into the house's entryway.

"In here," Jackson hollered back from the direction of the kitchen.

The second Lainie stepped into the room, several pairs of eyes shifted in her direction, but her focus was fixed solely on her son, who was seated at the kitchen table, eating an ice-cream cone. The only evidence that he'd been hurt was the twin trails the tears he'd shed had left on his dirty face.

She hurried over to him. "Are you okay? Where does it hurt?"

"Lainie," her brother said softly as he moved to stand beside her, "he's okay."

She shook her head. "We don't know that for sure.

Things happen. We should take him to an urgent care center or the emergency room to get looked at."

"Mom, I just tripped," Lucas said with an embarrassed frown. "That's all."

Blue, who was standing guard over her new friend, looked up at Lainie with those big green eyes of hers. "And he only cried a little bit."

"I didn't cry," Lucas grumbled. "My eyes watered 'cause I got dirt in them."

"That would make any man's eyes water," Jackson agreed.

"Oh, honey," Lainie groaned, hating that he was trying so hard to put up a tough front. Reaching down she touched gentle fingers to his scraped-up kneecap, made visible thanks to the oversize gym shorts he was wearing.

"Jessica couldn't tend to his wound through the tear in his jeans," Emma explained. "I found an old pair of Jackson's shorts for him to change into that would allow Jessica to see to his knee."

The tear? she thought with an inner wince. Oh, her poor baby. He must have hit the ground so hard. "Of course," she said shakily. "Thank you." She looked down at the angry red scratches and slight bruising on her son's kneecap. "We should go have this looked at."

"It looks worse than it is," a woman whose voice Lainie didn't recognize said softly.

Lainie glanced around, noting for the first time everyone that had gathered in the kitchen. Jackson, Tucker, Emma, Autumn, Justin, Blue and a pretty, very petite young woman she didn't recognize. She was dressed in white pants, white sneakers and what looked to be a scrub top with tiny pink and blue storks all over it. Her long blond hair was pulled back into a loose ponytail, and her light blue eyes were trained on Lucas.

The young woman smiled. "I looked him over and cleaned the dirt from his knee and both palms. He was able to put weight on that knee, and there's no swelling, only slight bruising, so I don't think anything is broken." She looked to Emma. "Mrs. Wade had some antibiotic ointment to put on the abrasions. He'll be tender for a few days, but he should heal up just fine."

"But his knee's so red," Lainie countered with a troubled frown. "I really think I need to take him somewhere to have it looked at."

"Lainie," Jackson said calmly, "this is Jessica Daniels." He motioned to the woman who had tended to her son. "She's a registered nurse."

"Hannah's friend," Lainie acknowledged.

"Yes," Jessica replied with a soft smile.

"Mom was on the phone talking to Hannah when I brought Lucas into the house. Jessica had just arrived to pick up her son and offered to run over and have a look at Lucas before heading back to the city."

Lainie looked to Jessica, feeling beyond grateful that she had taken the time to look in on Lainie's son. Her assurance that Lucas was all right helped to settle her frazzled nerves. "Thank you so much for taking care of my son."

"Yes," Justin chimed in with a charming grin, his gaze fixed on the woman who had come to his nephew's rescue, "thank you."

Jessica nodded. "You're welcome. I'm glad I could be of help."

"Lucas," Lainie prompted, "is there something you'd like to say to Mrs. Daniels?"

"Miss," the young woman corrected.

"Miss Daniels," Lainie repeated.

Her son's head bobbed up and down. "Thank you for taking care of me."

A smile spread across Jessica's face. "It was my pleasure. Do be careful when leaving the henhouse from here on out. Those ramps are better suited for itty-bitty chicken feet. I think to keep those pesky foxes away. You'll need to take your time and watch your step."

"I will," Lucas replied with a smile. He looked to Lainie. "Are we leaving now?"

"Shortly," she told him, wanting to express her gratitude as well before leaving.

"I need to get going," Jessica announced.

"Could I repay you with dinner this evening?" Lainie heard Justin call out to Jessica, drawing her attention back to the conversation going on around her. "For your help today," he added with a smile.

Lainie exchanged a surprised look with Jackson, who gave a slight shrug in response. They both knew Justin rarely took time for himself.

"Thank you for the invite," Jessica replied. "But Hannah's had Dustin far longer than she expected to have him today. We didn't know how badly Lucas was injured, so she insisted on keeping my son there until I was done seeing to your nephew. I really do need to go get him."

"There's a small Italian eatery that recently opened up at the edge of town, and I'm pretty sure they have a children's menu," her brother said with a charming grin and a determination Lainie had never seen in him before. "If you or Dustin don't care for Italian, I know a place that has really good burgers."

Jessica's gaze lowered to Justin's uniform. "Are you allowed to eat on duty?"

"It's not against the rules," he told her. "But it just so happens I got off duty about forty-five minutes ago."

And he wasn't heading home to catch up on some rest? Lainie looked to Jackson, who simply shrugged his own amazement at this unexpected turn of events.

"Ravioli?" Jessica inquired, her eyes reflecting more than a hint of interest in the invitation.

"The best," he answered.

"Well, I am hungry," she conceded.

"Then dinner it is," Justin replied with a victorious grin.

"I insist on paying for myself and my son," she said determinedly.

His grin wavered, but her brother managed to force it to remain intact. "I'm supposed to be taking you to dinner to show my appreciation for your having taken care of my nephew."

"Your company will be thanks enough," she told him. "In fact, it will be nice to have some adult dinner conversation for a change. Not that discussing the best techniques for catching the fattest fishing worms isn't entertaining."

Justin laughed. "No doubt. And I promise to avoid bringing up anything worm-related at dinner."

"I can't promise the same for Dustin," she told him. "Fishing is his favorite thing to do."

"You'll have to bring him over to the house sometime and fish in the river that runs through my property." He looked to Lucas. "The boys could fish together."

"I don't know how to," Lucas said with a pout.

"I'll teach you," Jackson volunteered. Then he looked to Lainie. "Or your mom can."

"My mom?" Lucas said, looking her way as if trying to imagine her actually fishing.

Jackson nodded. "Something tells me there are a lot of things you're going to find out your mom can do that you never imagined her doing. Like riding a horse or casting a fishing line."

It had been far too long since she'd last gone fishing. She assumed it would be like riding a bike—once you learned how you never forgot—but she couldn't know for sure. What she did remember was the fun she'd had doing so with her family. Fun her son should have the chance to experience for himself. "Jackson would be a much better teacher," Lainie said. "I could bait a hook and cast a line, but taking a fish off the line is something I never learned to do."

"It's never too late to learn," Jackson said with a grin and then turned his attention back to Lucas. "So how about it? Are you in?"

"Dustin would love to have a friend here to do things with," Jessica told him. "We're going to be moving to Bent Creek and he won't know anybody here."

"He knows me," Blue wasted no time in pointing out.

Jessica laughed softly. "Yes, he does. And you are his good friend. I should have said another friend would be nice."

Blue appeared satisfied with that response. She looked to Lucas. "We can all fish together."

"That would be fun," Lainie's son agreed with an excited grin. One would never guess he had taken a painful tumble not long before.

It was so good to see her son eager to participate in something she, too, had been invited to partake in. He'd shut her out for so long that even feeling the slightest crack in his emotional wall filled her with such hope. And to see him making new friends warmed her heart.

"Okay, so it's settled," Justin said, his grin stretching wide. "We'll set an afternoon aside just for fishing."

"Wanna go color?" Blue asked Lucas with a sweet smile.

"I'm too old to color," he told her.

Blue shook her head. "No, you're not. My daddy colors with me and he's old."

Autumn muffled a snicker.

"Not that old," Tucker said in his own defense. "But Blue's right. Anyone can color. There is no age limit."

Lucas eased his leg off the kitchen chair that it had been propped up on during Jessica's ministrations. "I suppose I could."

"I have a coloring book with dogs in it," Blue said with a triumphant smile.

Lucas stood, one hand gripping the oversize shorts to his waist. "Can I go out and swing on the tire swing after Blue and me are done?"

His request helped to calm Lainie's frazzled nerves even more. Clearly, her son had recovered from the traumatic tumble he'd taken in the chicken coop ramp. "You may."

"Thanks!" Lucas made his way out of the kitchen, limping ever so slightly.

"Me, too!" Blue exclaimed as she raced after him. "I like to swing!"

"I'd best go keep an eye on them," Tucker volunteered. "I'm good with a crayon. And I'm even better at swing pushing. Besides, one accident is enough for today." His lengthy strides carried him easily from the room.

One accident was enough for a lifetime, Lainie thought sadly. She sent a quick prayer of gratitude heavenward that Lucas hadn't been injured worse in the fall, as Jackson had been during his last and final rodeo. The memory of it had her sending up an additional prayer of thanks that Jackson hadn't suffered more serious, long-term injuries.

"Cover up with one of the throws while you're coloring," Emma called after them. "I don't want either of you catching a chill from lying on the living room floor." She looked to Lainie. "That's where Blue likes to color when she comes over here."

"I'm sure they'll be fine," Lainie said.

"As soon as Lucas's jeans are done in the dryer, we'll have him change back into them."

"Thank you for washing them," Lainie told Jackson's mother. "You didn't have to do that."

"I know, dear. But I've raised three boys. I'm used to tossing soiled clothes in the washer before the stains set in."

"Jessica," Lainie's brother said, "why don't I follow you to Garrett's place to get your son? Then you can follow me into town to the restaurant."

She nodded and then turned to Lainie. "Feel free to call me if you have any concerns. As a mother, I know how hard it is not to worry when your child is sick or injured."

That is true, Lainie thought to herself. But it was so much more than that. She had seen how quickly and unexpectedly someone she loved could be taken away. It was so hard to get past the fear of it happening to her again. "I will," she replied with a grateful smile. "Maybe we'll have a chance to meet up under better circumstances since we'll both be living here. Especially since our boys are so close in age."

"I'd like that."

"I can think of a better circumstance," Autumn said, drawing their attention her way. "Hannah and I are working with Reverend Walker to put together a gift basket drive for the less fortunate during the holidays. It would be nice to have a couple more volunteers to help with the collecting and then the delivery of them to those families. Although Jessica, I know it might be hard for you with your work schedule to fit it in."

"I can work it in," Jessica replied. "Dustin can help me with the collecting."

"Or you can leave him here when you girls head into town to speak to the store owners," Emma suggested. "Blue and Lucas, too."

"I can't ask you to do that," Jessica said, shaking her head.

"You didn't," Jackson's mother said. "I offered. I miss having children around now that my boys had to go and grow up into big, strapping men."

Everyone around her was so kind and giving. Lainie couldn't help but be touched by it all. And to think that she would have the opportunity to be a part of that giving, well, it just made her feel so good inside.

"We're trying to fill that void by giving you plenty of grandchildren to fuss over," Tucker said with a grin. "At least, Garrett and I are. Jackson's still trying to find a woman capable of making him want to settle down."

"Everyone finds love in their own time," Emma replied. "Love has no time limit."

Lainie knew that all too well. Even after all these years, after all the hurt, she still had love in her heart for Jackson. A love that seemed to be growing stronger since coming back, much to her dismay.

"Emma is serious," Autumn told Jessica. "She's happier than a kitten with a ball of yarn when she has children here for her to fawn over."

"If you're sure," Jessica replied and then turned to Autumn, "then you count me in."

"Great," Autumn replied. "I'll let Hannah know. Or, better yet, you can tell her when you pick up Dustin."

"It's so kind of you girls to think of others this way," Emma said, a bit misty eyed.

Lainie felt her own eyes tearing up.

"I know times are hard for some," Jackson's mother went on. "And the holidays can be a painful reminder of that. More so this year since Wilmot Manufacturing closed its doors over in Bilmont. Several people from church alone had been employed there. I'll tell you what," she said thoughtfully. "Put Grady and me down for two holiday gift basket donations."

"I'll put a basket together," Justin offered without hesitation.

Lainie had to wonder when her brother was going to find time to put his donation together with his busy work schedule, but then he was making time for dinner with Jessica and her son. She just prayed he didn't intend to burn the candle at both ends in the process.

"I'm in for a couple," Jackson said. "Just tell me what you'd like in them."

"The letter we've sent out to local businesses suggests baskets filled with toys, nonperishable food, housewares, gift cards, anything a family in need might be able to use," Autumn explained. "The reverend is putting together a list of names for us and we'll deliver the gift baskets to those families Christmas Eve morning."

Lainie felt blessed to know such kindhearted people. And what a wonderful thing to do, helping those in need. She would love nothing more than to be a part of it. "I'd love to help out," she said, "but I don't drive. I'd be happy to donate one though."

"Nonsense," Autumn said with a dismissive wave. "Not that a basket donation wouldn't be appreciated. But there's no reason you can't help out. You can just ride with us when we go out to collect the contributions, and then when we deliver the baskets as well. On top of being emotionally rewarding, it'll be more fun with all of us doing this together."

"I'd like very much to be a part of your holiday basket collection," Lainie told them. It was something she intended to put her whole heart into, wanting to give back to the town that gave so much to her growing up. To help those in need, because she knew firsthand how it felt to need help but not be able to bring yourself to ask for it. "It will be so nice to be a part of something again. A part of this town, helping others. And it will give me a chance to renew old acquaintances and friendships." Maybe even take a step closer to the faith she used to hold so dear.

"This is wonderful," Autumn said, her face alight with joy. "I'll call Reverend Walker this evening and let him know."

Jessica said her goodbyes and then left.

Justin looked to Lainie. "You and Lucas are welcome to join us."

"I…" She looked to Jackson and then back to her brother. "We already have plans. I made a chicken casserole this morning to stick in the oven this evening and invited Jackson to join us when I dropped Lucas off earlier. I wasn't sure if you would be home or not, but I made enough for everyone."

Justin asked, "You invited Jackson to dinner?"

She shifted uneasily. "To pay him back for giving Lucas riding lessons," Lainie said, feeling the need to explain her reason for extending a dinner invite to Jackson. "I thought you were working this evening."

"Sam Collins has agreed to come back part-time and has been helping out some this week. He'll continue to do so until Deputy Mitchell gets back."

"I thought Sam was working with his dad now." Although he had worked for the sheriff's department a few years earlier, he'd left to help his father with the family business.

"He is," her brother said. "But construction is slow right now over the holidays and Sam already knows the ropes. It'll give Vance and I a little bit of a breather to say the least. And I'll get to spend more time with you and Lucas."

Which meant she would be spending less time with Jackson. Lainie knew she should be relieved. But instead she felt awash in sadness. She forced a smile. "That'll be great."

"I'd best get going," her brother said. "I wouldn't want Jessica to think I changed my mind." Leaning in, he kissed her cheek, waved goodbye to the others and then hurried from the room.

As soon as he had gone, Lainie turned to Jackson, Autumn and Emma. "Can somebody please tell me what just happened here?"

Jackson chuckled. "I'd say your brother finally had his head turned by the right woman."

Emma's head bobbed in agreement. "He did seem quite taken with Jessica."

"I don't know why we never thought to introduce the two of them to each other," Autumn muttered.

Lainie shook her head. "I've never seen him like that before. Don't get me wrong. His job, when it's not crazy stressful like it is right now, makes him happy. But this is a far different kind of happy."

"He was definitely bound and determined to take Jessica to dinner," Jackson muttered.

"And her son," Autumn pointed out. "Jessica has had issues in the past with men not offering to include her son."

"Justin would never leave her son out," Lainie said. "But then my brother would tend to be more empathetic to someone in her situation, his having a sister who is also raising her young son alone."

Emma nodded in agreement. "You should have seen the look on your brother's face when he rushed into the kitchen after getting your call and found Jessica kneeling on the floor beside Lucas, cleaning his wounds. He nearly stumbled over his own booted feet."

"Well, if he wasn't such a workaholic, he might have met Jessica at Hannah and Garrett's wedding," Jackson said. "Who knows? Maybe he'll finally discover that there's more to life than work."

"That would be nice," Lainie said. "He deserves to be happy."

"So do you," Jackson said, meeting her gaze.

Only the Lord knew what His plans for her were. She just prayed that happiness was a part of the future He was guiding her toward.

Chapter Six

Jackson knocked again, a little louder than before and then glanced around. No sign of Lainie or Lucas outside. Maybe her parents had come by to pick them up and take them somewhere. He didn't have any set plans with Lainie and her son. It had just become habit to swing by and check on them each day after his work was done at the ranch. And he wanted to see how Lucas's knee was mending, now that a few days had gone by since his fall. Turning, he had just started for the porch steps when Justin's front door swung open.

"Sorry," Lainie said, her breathing slightly labored. A single strand of hair hung down over her eyes, her ponytail drooping slightly off-center at the back of her head. "I was up searching in the attic."

"Lucas ran off to the attic?"

"No," she said, looking confused by his words. "He went with Mom and Dad for the day."

"Why didn't you go with them?" he asked. Not that it was any of his business.

"Because I had things to do here. Like find my

brother's missing limbs, which I have been searching for in the attic for well over an hour."

He blinked. "Justin is missing his limbs?"

Lainie laughed softly. "Tree limbs," she clarified. "I was going to put up his artificial Christmas tree for him, which, according to my brother, he hasn't put up since our parents sold him the house, but not all of the branches were in the box. Thus the search. I know it's not as special as a real tree, but at least it would be something."

Jackson nodded knowingly. "It appears you've been up there longer than an hour. Long enough, at least, for a spider to spin its web in your hair."

Her hands flew to her head, swiping at her hair. "Ooh! Get it off me!" she shrieked. Lainie had always hated spiders.

He calmly reached out to pluck a shimmery strand of cobweb from her hair and held it up for her to see. "All gone," he assured her with a grin.

She let out a sigh of relief. "Thank you."

"Anytime."

She stepped aside. "Come on in. Just excuse my disheveled appearance."

"No excuse needed. Dust looks good on you," he told her.

"Thank you," she said. "I think."

"Definitely a compliment," he told her as he followed her into the living room, where a partially erected Christmas tree stood in the corner. What limbs there were shot out at all sorts of odd angles.

Lainie, who now stood next to Jackson, eyeing the misshapen tree, leaned his way. "Thus the search for the missing limbs."

He looked her way, taking in her pretty smile and bright eyes. "Would you like some help searching for them?"

"If I hadn't already gone through the attic inch by inch, I would be more than happy to have your assistance in finding the rest of the Christmas tree, but I know for a fact that there are no more branches up there." She released a frustrated sigh. "They must've been stored away in more than one box and were accidentally thrown out when Justin was spring cleaning last year."

"Something tells me it wasn't by accident," Jackson told her. "Your brother's not really into decorating for the holidays. Mostly because he's too busy to take the time to do so. But I've also heard him say that Christmas trees are meant for families to enjoy, and since he's a confirmed bachelor there's really no need for him to have one."

"He's said the same thing to me before, too," she admitted. "But I honestly don't think he realizes part of the tree is missing. Or he wouldn't have told Lucas and I to feel free to put it up since we were going to be living here over the holidays."

"Why isn't Lucas here helping you?" he said. "If you don't mind my asking."

She averted her gaze. "He said a tree wouldn't make his Christmas any better. I just thought that if I put one up, maybe, just maybe, he would remember the joy the holiday had once brought him. When I was up in the attic sorting through the Christmas decorations, Lucas called my dad and asked if they would come get him for the afternoon. When they showed up to get him, much to my surprise, Dad said Lucas had told them I was busy doing things and that he was bored."

"I take it you didn't say otherwise," he said with a frown.

She shook her head. "I don't want my parents to worry about us any more than they already do. Besides, the therapist I'd taken my son to told me the emotional healing takes time."

A loss they both had suffered, yet, Lainie, loving mother that she was, did all she could to stay strong and shoulder the burden of her son's anger, of his pushing her away, of having to start her life all over again— alone. He wanted so much at that moment to hold her. To tell her that everything would be all right, that he would do everything in his power to make it all right. Instead, he settled for saying, "I can only imagine how hard the holidays must be for Lucas. For you as well."

Lainie had fallen silent, making Jackson want, more than anything, to put a smile back on her pretty face.

"Well," he muttered as he stood there eyeing up the tree, "you can't very well celebrate the holiday with half a tree." He turned to her. "Go get your coat."

"My coat?" she repeated, her gaze lifting to meet his. "For what?"

"We're going to find you a Christmas tree. One with perfect branches just waiting to have popcorn garlands strung all over them."

"We don't have any popcorn garlands," she told him.

"An easy fix," he said with a grin. "Now get your coat and meet me outside." With that, Jackson headed outside to his truck to get his work gloves, shoving them into his coat pockets. Then he grabbed the bow saw he kept in the oversize toolbox in the bed of his truck and placed it atop the rubber floor mat behind the passenger seat.

A few moments later, Lainie joined him outside. She was bundled in her charcoal woolen coat with a thick knit plaid scarf wrapped around her neck. "I haven't gone to pick out a real Christmas tree since I was a young girl," she said with a smile as she pulled on a pair of bright red gloves that matched the plaid in her scarf. She'd taken her hair out, freeing it to hang loose about her slender shoulders. A dark gray knit cap sat atop her head. She looked right at home in the December chill that filled the Wyoming air. And beautiful. But then Lainie had always been beautiful to him.

"That's the only kind of tree to have as far as I'm concerned," Jackson said with a grin. "Unless someone has issues with pine allergies, of course."

"Thankfully, no allergies in our family," she replied. "For which I am so grateful. I've always loved the smell of fresh-cut pine."

"Then we're good to go." The moment she started for the passenger-side door, he cut her off. "You're driving."

Her panicked gaze snapped up to his. "What?"

"It's time for you to get back into the saddle, Lainie," he said, his tone tender.

Shaking her head and taking a step back, she said, "Jackson, I can't."

"You can," he said reassuringly. "We're only going down the road to my place. It's a short drive."

Her gaze darted to the truck and then to the distant road.

"Lainie, you need to be able to get places. Not that anyone minds giving you a ride somewhere when you need it. But there will be times you need to get somewhere and might not be able to find someone available to take you. To the store, to your parents' place for a visit, to school functions or, God forbid, if an emergency of some sort arises." He met her troubled gaze. "You need to take back your life."

"I know that," she said. "I want to. I'm just not sure I can. Not after…" Her words trailed off.

"Let me help you," he said softly.

"What if I pass a car and panic?"

"The only traffic you're going to get on this road would be my family," he reminded her. "And if you panic we'll deal with it. I'll be right beside you."

"Will was beside me," she said.

"Lainie, that accident wasn't your fault. You were hit by a drunk driver," he said calmly. "Don't let that person's mistake take away any more from you than it already has." He held out the fob with his truck key dangling from it. "Trust me?"

"Yes," she said, her fingers closing around the key.

Jackson walked her around to the driver's side and then helped her up onto the seat. "Proud of you, Lainie Girl." Closing the door, he made his way around to the passenger side and settled himself into the dark leather bucket seat.

"Make sure you put your seat belt on," she said anxiously.

"Always do," he assured her with a grin. "I believe in being safe."

"Will was wearing a seat belt that night," she said, her words a mere whisper. "It didn't keep him safe." Pulling her hands from the wheel, she covered her face. "I can't do this, Jackson. Not with you in here."

"You can do it," he countered calmly.

Lowering her trembling hands, she looked his way, tears looming in her eyes. "I don't want anything to happen to you."

"You're a good driver, Lainie," he told her. "I don't have the slightest reservation getting into a car with you. Besides, my not riding with you won't change anything if it's my time to go. Lord willing, however, I'll be around for a very long time."

"In the logical part of my mind, I know what you're saying is true," she replied with a frown. "It's the illogical part of my mind I need to set at ease." Determined to try to push past this life-altering fear, one that had affected both her and her son, Lainie knew she had to force herself to drive again. "Would you mind if I said a little prayer before we set out?"

"You never have to ask my permission to seek comfort in prayer."

She closed her eyes and said, "Lord, please keep Jackson and me safe as we travel down the road together." Request made, she opened her eyes and inserted the key he'd given her into the ignition and, with a slight turn, started the engine. Then she took hold of the steering wheel, flexing her fingers tentatively around it, as if trying to gather up her courage to take the wheel fully in hand. "My heart is beating so fast," she said with a nervous laugh.

"That's because you're sitting beside me," he said with a teasing grin.

She shot him a sidelong glance before shaking her head, a hint of a smile returning to her face. "It's a wonder no woman has managed to snag you yet."

Maybe because he hadn't wanted any other woman.

It had always been her. Not that he hadn't dated here and there. But no one else had been able to compete with the woman who had lodged herself into his heart. And then, after his accident, he'd pretty much stopped dating altogether, placing all of his focus on the family's rodeo business.

"We'd best get going," Jackson said. "It might take a while to find the right tree."

Lainie took a deep breath and then reached for the gearshift, putting it in Drive. Then she pulled slowly away from her brother's house. By the time they reached the road at the end of the long gravel drive, the tension in her shoulders had visibly lessened, easing some of Jackson's guilt for pushing her to do something she feared doing.

"It's been a long time since I've sat behind the wheel of a car," she said. "But even longer since I drove a pickup truck."

"Probably not much call for them in the city."

She shook her head as they made their way down the road.

"You okay?" Jackson asked, after an extended silence. He prayed he had done the right thing in pushing Lainie to confront her fears. He'd like to think he would have done the same had he been physically capable of riding a bull again.

"Yes," she replied. "I can't explain it, but for some reason I feel safe up here inside this oversize ranch truck."

He grinned. "I'd like to think some of that has to do with having a big, strong cowboy seated next to you."

"That, too," she allowed, her smile widening a little bit farther.

When they pulled up the drive to his place and came to a stop next to his barn, Lainie put the car into Park and then turned to him with a beaming smile. "I did it," she said, sounding equal amounts shocked and elated.

The corners of Jackson's mouth hitched. "That's my girl."

Their gazes met for a long moment before she looked away, pinning hers on the road ahead. "It's been so long. I never thought I would be able to get behind the wheel of a car ever again, but sitting in the driver's seat of this truck, I felt…"

"Strong," he answered for her. "Like you're taking back control of your life."

She nodded, her hazel eyes lifting to meet his searching gaze. "Do you think we could do this again sometime? Maybe try going a little farther?"

"Hmm… I'll have to think that one over a bit," he said, pretending to contemplate her question. "Getting you back behind the wheel would mean I would no longer be needed to take you and Lucas here and there. I'm not so sure I'm ready to give that up."

"I would think you would be relieved," she told him with a smile.

"You'd be wrong."

Her smile softened with his admission. "I'm realistic, if anything. I know I have a long way to go before I'm going to be comfortable behind the wheel, but I want my independence back. Want to be the kind of mother Lucas deserves."

His expression softened even more. "Your son is already blessed to have you for his mother, whether you drive or not. He's just too young to really appreciate what he has, but that will come. Right now, he's still working through a lot of pain and grief."

Reaching over, she covered his hand with hers, giving it a squeeze. "I've missed you, Jackson Wade."

He chuckled. "You see me every day."

"I've missed having you in my life," she admitted with a soft smile. "If I could turn back time…"

"I've missed you, too." More than she would ever know. "And if there was a way to change the past, I would. At least, to where we parted on better terms." Withdrawing his hand before he confessed feelings better off kept tucked safely away, he opened his door. "And just so you know, what you did today took courage. Proud of you, Lainie Girl. Now, let's go find you a tree."

They stepped out of the truck, Jackson collecting the bow saw and a tarp, along with some rope to bind the tree for their return trip. Then they set off together around the side of Jackson's house and across the backyard toward the expanse of pines and other trees that lined it. A light dusting of freshly fallen snow coated the ground and trees, sparkling under the afternoon sun.

"Tell me when you see a tree you like," he told Lainie.

"I don't know how I'm ever going to decide," she said, her gaze sweeping the scattering of pines around them. "There are so many to choose from."

"I think we need a really big one," he suggested. "One with really wide, full limbs."

"Justin would just love that, I'm sure," she said with a playful roll of her eyes.

"Exactly," he agreed. "It'll make up for all the years he's gone without a tree."

She laughed. "Are you trying to get me evicted from my temporary home?"

He pushed aside a tree branch that was blocking their way, allowing Lainie to pass through before following close behind her. "Not a chance of that happening. Your brother loves you." *I love you.*

Jackson nearly tripped over his own two feet with that realization, his bad leg requiring a bit more effort to right himself.

Lainie turned with a soft gasp, her hand reaching out to steady him, to keep him from taking a nosedive across the pine needle–strewn ground below. "I've got you."

I've got you. Her words had embarrassment spiking heat to his cheeks. Her instinctual reaction to his stumble was a reminder of how Lainie and others saw him now—no longer the fully capable man he'd once been. His physical imperfection set him apart from the other men he knew. And it would never change.

Just as his feelings for her wouldn't. He loved Lainie. Not the love of friends who had grown up together like siblings, but a deep, heart-swelling kind of love that could only lead to more complications for her if he were to act upon those carefully restrained feelings. Lainie deserved the best, and, as far as Jackson was concerned, he was no longer eligible for the list of men who were best for Lainie. He was lame and scarred, and no longer the rodeo cowboy she had once been so starry-eyed over. Even something as simple as racing each other across the pastures on foot as they once had done was impossible. Now, for him to do so would cause him more than a fair amount of discomfort. Lainie deserved a man who could run and laugh with her. He wasn't that man.

He eased free of her grip. "I'm fine," he muttered.

"Jackson, I…"

"Let's find that tree," he said, moving on. Only now he was more conscious of his awkward gait than ever before.

Lainie hurried to catch up with him. "I'm sorry. I never meant to—"

He stopped abruptly, causing her apology to falter. Turning to face her, he said sharply, "Let's get the elephant out of the room." His gaze swept about their surroundings. "Or in our case, the woods." He looked down into Lainie's eyes. "I've got a bum leg. No changing that. But I'm still capable of righting myself after a minor off-step. I don't need your help or anyone else's to stand on my own two feet."

Hurt filled her hazel eyes. "Of course, you don't," she replied. "I just reacted the way I would have for anyone I thought was about to fall. It had nothing to do with your leg."

He realized the truth in her words. Lainie would help anyone in need. Except for herself. That's what he was supposed to do—be the person for her to lean on. How was she supposed to trust him to be that for her when he refused to allow her to do the same for him? *Lord, please help me to set aside my pride to accept the things I can't change.*

"Lainie," he said, taking her hands in his, "I'm the one who's sorry. Sometimes my pride gets the better of me. I shouldn't have taken my frustration out on you." His gaze lifted from their joined hands to her eyes. "I tripped. Anyone would have reacted the way you did. I would have done the same thing, whether it was you or one of my brothers." He smiled. "Even if it were old Mrs. Wilkins, who smells like a perfume factory. And I can tell you from experience that anyone who so much as even sits next to her ends up smelling like one, too."

A tiny smile pulled at her lips, easing some of Jackson's guilt. "In church?" she asked, a hint of humor now lighting her hazel eyes.

He nodded. "Yep. She's a sweet old woman, but I have to say that was the longest sermon I ever sat through. My eyes were watering like crazy, and I found myself fighting to hold back the sneeze of all sneezes. My determination won out and I made it to my truck before launching into a fit of achoos."

Lainie giggled and it was as if the sun had suddenly pushed aside the dull gray clouds that filled the winter sky. "I remember sitting by her a few times growing up. I seem to recall her being partial to lavender- and gardenia-based perfumes."

"Your memory serves you well," he said with a nod. "Now, am I forgiven?"

Lainie smiled up at Jackson, taking in his handsome face, slightly pinkened from the cold, the icy flakes of snow clinging to his deep chestnut hair. He was so much more than the boy she had fallen in love with all those years ago. He was taller, broader, prouder. More handsome than any man had a right to be. And his heart was as large and giving as the land around them.

As much as she tried to fight it since coming to Bent Creek, she seemed to be doing a backslide into the past. She was falling for Jackson all over again. No, not over again. She had never fully stopped loving him, if she was honest with herself. But she wouldn't jeopardize their newly rekindled friendship by giving in to her heart's desire. "You're forgiven."

The worry creases at the edges of his eyes eased as he stood looking down at her. "I'm glad. I don't ever want to be at odds with you ever again. Our friendship is way too important to me."

"To me as well," she said softly, her heart yearning for so much more.

He shifted the bow saw to his other hand. "Best get back to our tree hunt before you turn into a walking, talking icicle. It's cold out here."

"That won't be a problem," she told him. "Our hunt is over."

Confusion lit his gaze. "I thought I was forgiven."

"You are." The smile on her face broadened. "Our hunt is over, because I think I found our Christmas tree."

His brows lifted. "You did?"

She pointed past him to an impressive Norway spruce that stood well over six feet in height and had full, nearly perfect branches. Then she looked to Jackson. "Do you think it's too big for the living room?"

He walked over to it to size it up. "It's tall, but I think you'll have a little room to spare as far as the ceiling is concerned." He circled the tree. "Nice shape to it." She watched as he ran a branch through his enclosed hand to make certain the needles held firm. Then he gave a nod of approval. "Good choice."

"I'm not so sure it is now that I see how big this tree is when you're standing next to it."

He glanced up at the tree's pointed tip and then back

at Lainie. "It's a big one. I'll give you that. But it's also meant to be a Christmas tree. They're supposed to be tall. That way, everyone can look up to admire the star perched atop it."

"I never thought of it that way, but you're right. Nothing warms a heart and brings on a feeling of inner peace more than when you're looking up at a lit Christmas tree, its star shining ever-so-brightly overhead."

"Just to clarify before I start cutting," he said. "This is definitely *the one*, right?"

"Yes," she said, excitement lacing her tone.

"Okay," he said with a nod as he pulled his leather work gloves from his coat pockets and slid them on. He glanced her way. "After I trim away some of the bottom branches to give us a base for the tree stand, I'll need you to help support the tree while I cut through its trunk."

"Okay," she said, reaching out to take hold of one of the thicker lower branches. She'd helped her dad and brother many a holiday as they cut down their chosen Christmas tree. The first time they'd gone tree hunting with her family, she'd cried, not wanting to cut down the beautiful pine they'd chosen. Then her father explained that it wasn't a bad thing. Thinning wooded areas helped the remaining trees grow stronger, as they constantly had to compete for soil and sunlight. It also allowed for the growth of more plants along the ground floor, offering more food and shelter to the wildlife. One thing Lainie loved more than the trees when she was little were the animals that made the woods their home.

Jackson knelt at the base of the tree and began to remove its lowest branches. Once he had them cleared away, he said, "I'll cut as low to the ground as possible."

"To better the chance of the remaining trunk resprouting and forming another future Christmas tree," she said knowingly. So much of her past that she had set aside was coming back to her now. Like how incredibly soothing it was to be surrounded by God's beautiful land, with its wide, open skies and tall, thick trees. And then there were the memory-prodding scents of pine and earth. A soft, contented sigh passed her lips.

Jackson shifted to grin up at her, past the bushy branches. "You can take the country girl out of the city, but she's always going to be a country girl at heart." Then he disappeared under the bushy bottom branches and began sawing into the spruce's thick trunk.

Once the final cut was made, Jackson stood and took hold of the tree, relieving Lainie of her duty. "That didn't take long." Stepping back, she brushed a few stray spruce needles from the sleeve of her jacket.

"I've had a lot of years to practice," he said with a grin. He gave the tree a firm shake to free it of any bugs or spiders that might have taken up residence in its branches for the winter months and then had Lainie open the tarp that they had brought along with them.

Twenty minutes later, they had the tree loaded and Lainie was driving them back to her brother's house. That was her idea. While she wasn't completely comfortable yet, she had to believe it would be more so in time. Prayed it would. After pulling up to the house, she and Jackson carried the bundled-up spruce into Justin's house. "I wish Lucas could have gone with us," Lainie said with a sigh.

"Maybe next year he'll join us," Jackson said as they navigated their way into the living room.

Next year. She liked the thought of Jackson being a part of her future holidays. Even if it were only as a friend.

Needing a moment to herself, she said, "I'll run up to the attic and grab Mom and Dad's old Christmas tree stand." Made specifically for real trees, it contained a large water reservoir.

"I'll disassemble the old tree, or what there is of it, and then get the tarp off this one while you're doing that."

"Sounds like a plan." Turning away, she hurried up the stairs and then up into the attic, where she sat down against the wall and closed her eyes in silent prayer. *Dear Lord, please give me the strength to keep Jackson safe from my love.* And then she added a prayer for her son. *I pray You will help Lucas navigate another holiday and the pain it brings him now that his father is gone. Amen.*

"Lainie?"

Her head popped up at the sound of Jackson's voice. She scrambled to her feet. "I'll be down in a moment," she called back as she hurried over to the old tree stand.

The attic stairs creaked as Jackson joined her. "I didn't know if you needed help bringing anything else down."

She'd already carried the boxes of ornaments downstairs. Looking around, her gaze came to rest on another container that had evidently seen a lot of Christmases. "Can you grab that one?" she said, pointing to it. "The tree lights are in there, along with the star. Although I'm not sure if they even work anymore."

"I guess we'll find out," he said, ducking his head to avoid hitting the low-hanging ceiling as he crossed the room. He lifted the heavy box with ease and then turned. "After you."

Heavy metal tree stand in hand, she made her way downstairs. She went to get a pitcher of water while Jackson secured the tree she'd chosen in the stand. When Lainie returned, she paused in the doorway to admire the Norway spruce standing tall and proud in the far corner of the room. "Couldn't be more perfect," she said in admiration of her chosen tree. But it had been more than choosing a pine tree for the Christmas holiday that had been perfect. It had been facing her fear of getting behind the wheel of a car again. It had been spending time with Jackson and feeling some of that closeness they had once shared. It had been taking back some of the pieces of herself that had been lost for so many years.

Jackson paused in the midst of stringing the Christmas lights to glance her way with a grin. "Not always. But I try."

Laughter spilled from her lips as she crossed the room to join him. "I was referring to the tree," she said as she bent to fill the reservoir with water. "But you do come in a close second when it comes to being perfect."

Silence followed.

Lainie straightened and turned to face Jackson. His gaze was fixed on his bad leg. His playful grin had slipped a notch. Reaching up, she cupped his cheek. "You are perfect," she said, refusing to allow his insecurity when it came to his leg to take away from the incredible man he was.

"Lainie..." he said tenderly, leaning in as if to kiss her.

Her heart leaped. Was she ready for this? Did she even want him to kiss her? As she leaned in to meet him, she knew in that moment she did.

A cell phone rang.

Hers. Blushing, Lainie pulled back and hurried over to where she'd left her purse lying when they'd returned home. "Hello?" she said, grateful for the interruption. Otherwise, she might have let Jackson kiss her, something she wasn't so sure she was prepared for now that she'd had a moment to step away.

"Mom…" her son said on the other end of the line.

He didn't sound upset, but that didn't lessen the worry she felt when she asked, "Is everything okay?"

"Mom," he said with a groan, "why do you always have to ask me that?"

Maybe because he hadn't been okay. Not for a very long time. Throw in the fear of losing Lucas as she had his father. Suddenly. Irrevocably.

Jackson moved to stand beside her.

Lainie signaled to him that everything was all right and then returned her focus to the conversation. "Because I'm a mother, and it's my job to worry. So what's up?"

"Grandma was talking to Uncle Justin on the phone and he said that he was taking that lady who fixed my knee and her son to dinner and the movies. He asked if I'd like to go with them. Can I, Mom? Please?"

Justin was taking Jessica to the movies? Well, well. It appeared her brother was verging on being completely smitten. Dinner, and now a movie *and* dinner. "I'll have to talk to your uncle first."

"He's going to be calling you," her son said. "I just wanted to tell you that I'd really like to go."

Other than his joy at the horse-riding lessons he'd been having with Jackson, this was the most excited she'd heard her son in a very long time. She couldn't hold back her smile. Her son's happiness meant the world to her. Since he was finding it in so many things since coming home, Lainie knew she had made the right decision in moving back to Bent Creek. "If Jessica and her son don't mind, then, yes, you can go."

"Thanks, Mom!"

Her phone buzzed, signaling another incoming call. Lainie glanced at the screen. "Uncle Justin is calling. I'll see what's going on and call you back after I've talked to him."

"Okay," her son said excitedly. "Love you!" A second later, the line went dead.

Tears of joy nearly sprang to her eyes. When was the last time her son had spoken those words to her? She answered her brother's call. "Hello?"

"Hey, sis," he said. "I'm heading over to pick Jessica and her son up when I get off work this afternoon. We're going to the movies and then grabbing a bite to eat afterward."

"I know."

"You know?"

"Lucas just called."

"Beat me to it, did he?" he said with a chuckle.

"He did at that."

"Would you mind if he went with us?" her asked. "We're going to be right down the road from Mom and Dad's place, so it wouldn't be any trouble to swing by and pick Lucas up."

"Have you checked with Jessica to make certain he wouldn't be imposing on your date?"

"Already ran it by her," her brother replied. "She's more than okay with it. And who said anything about this being a date?"

She laughed, her gaze following Jackson as he returned to stringing the Christmas lights on the tree, no doubt wanting to give her a modicum of privacy. "Has it been so long since you were on a date that you don't remember what one is? Asking a woman out to dinner could fall under that category. Asking her out again, this time to a movie and dinner, definitely sounds like a date to me."

"Dinner was repayment for tending to Lucas when he was injured," he explained. "And this evening… well, it's for the kids. Something to do while they're on Christmas break from school."

"I see," she said, her gaze shifting to Jackson. "So then you wouldn't mind if I invited Jessica to come over and help Jackson and I string popcorn for the tree while you take the boys to the movies?"

Her brother hesitated, and then with a heavy sigh said, "All right, I like her. And yes, I would mind."

She let out a soft giggle. "Figured as much. Maybe you could bring Jessica and Austin back here afterward. They could help us make the popcorn garland."

"I'll ask her, but she works the early shift tomorrow. I'd imagine she'll need to head home after dinner."

"Probably so," Lainie agreed.

"Maybe some other time. Getting back to stringing popcorn garland," he said, "I take it that means I now have a Christmas tree up somewhere in my house."

"You do," she replied with a smile. "Several of them, in fact. One in each room."

"Lainie," he choked out.

She laughed again, and it felt so good. There had been a time when she wondered if she would ever even smile again, let alone laugh out loud. Coming home had not only helped her son to start to heal emotionally, it was helping her as well. "I'm teasing," she told him. "There's only one and I picked it out myself. Well, not exactly myself. I couldn't have gotten it without Jackson's help. We drove over to his place to find a tree and then he cut it down for me."

"*You* put up a real tree?" her brother said in surprise. "I thought you were all about faux trees since moving to California."

"Will preferred artificial trees," she replied, feeling both sad and guilty at the mention of his name in the same room where she'd nearly kissed Jackson.

"I'm sorry, sis," her brother said regretfully. "I didn't mean to stir up painful memories."

"Don't apologize," she told him. "Will was Lucas's father. I have no intention of setting aside the memories we have of him just because it might be painful at times. Now, getting back to the movie non-date you are taking Jessica and her son on. If you're sure she doesn't mind, then Lucas can go with you."

"Great. I'll bring him home with me and save Mom and Dad a trip. And who knows, maybe Jessica and her son will be able to join us."

Save them a trip. If she could bring herself to drive without having Jackson at her side, then nobody would have to go out of their way to run her and Lucas to and fro. It had been so much easier to get around in Sacramento between walking and, when necessary, a taxi. Thankfully, almost everything they had needed had been within walking distance. And the weather hadn't really ever been an issue. Jackson was right. It was time she pushed her fears aside and got back up on that proverbial horse for good.

"That would be nice," she said. "I'll call Lucas back to let him know."

"No need," her brother said. "Truth is, I'm looking forward to spending some time with him now that my work schedule is easing up a bit, thanks to Sam coming back part-time."

"I know he's been wanting to spend time with you, even though he understands why you haven't been around much."

"You can't imagine how guilty I feel about leaving you and Lucas high and dry since your return," Justin replied, regret clear in his voice.

"You didn't leave us high and dry. You made sure we had Jackson looking after us," she reminded him. Though she'd been against the arrangement in the beginning, she was now beyond grateful for the time she and Jackson had been able to spend together. It had helped to heal the rift between them.

"Good news is, I can now let Jackson off the hook," her brother added.

Her heart sank a little at the thought. While she was happy to finally be able to spend time with her brother, not seeing Jackson every day was almost painful. "I'm sure he'll be relieved to get his walking papers," she said, casting a glance in Jackson's direction. "Talk to you when you get home."

Shoving her phone back into her purse, she crossed the room and bent to open one of the ornament storage boxes. *His walking papers.* Jackson would be free to go back to his life as usual. While she would have to get used to hers without him in it as much.

"Something on your mind?"

She glanced up at Jackson. "I was just thinking about my brother." *And you.*

"Something wrong?" he asked.

"Justin has a date this evening."

"I heard," he admitted. "Not that I meant to pry."

"I would have stepped out of the room if I hadn't wanted my conversation overheard," she assured him as she began busying herself with unwrapping more ornaments, which she placed atop the coffee table to keep them safe until they could be hung.

He studied her for a long moment. "Are you okay with him taking Jessica out?"

She met his questioning gaze. "Why wouldn't I be?"

"I might be reading something into this that's not there, but you don't seem overly happy about it. Is it because Justin's time is finally freeing up, but he's spending it elsewhere instead of with you and Lucas."

She shook her head. "That's not it at all. Justin and I have managed to find time to visit between his demanding work shifts. I would never begrudge him for taking time for himself. Truth is, I can't even recall the last time my brother went out on a real date."

He nodded. "Work does take up a lot of his time."

"He needs this," she said with a tender smile. "I want it for him. But a part of me worries that my brother is too busy to be the settling-down type. You and I both know he's always joked about being dedicated to bachelorhood."

Grabbing a handful of smaller bulbs, Jackson began hanging them from the branches at the top of the tree.

"Since he became sheriff, his career has definitely taken top priority in his life. And it shows. He's good at what he does, is well respected by both his employees and those who live here in Bent Creek, but that doesn't mean he can't have a change of heart where bachelorhood is concerned."

And what about Jackson? He hadn't wanted a serious relationship when they were younger, and he had yet to put down marital roots. Would he ever have a change of heart where his bachelorhood was concerned? Lainie pulled another tissue-wrapped ornament from the box and began peeling away its protective covering. "I hope you're right. I would hate to see Jessica end up getting hurt."

Jackson stopped what he was doing to glance over his broad shoulder at her. "Your brother's as good as they come. Always putting others before himself. What makes you think he would hurt her?"

Because she knew firsthand that even good guys were capable of hurting a woman who cared about them. "I don't think he would intentionally. But he's so used to putting his job before everything else. And you and I both know he's never been a long-term commitment type of guy when it comes to relationships."

"Maybe that's because the right woman hadn't come along yet," he surmised.

"For Justin's sake, I pray she is the right woman for my brother," Lainie said as she stepped forward to hang a red-and-green glass bulb from one of the lower limbs. "For Jessica's sake, I hope he decides quickly if this thing between them has the potential to go long-term or not. Because it's not just Jessica who is investing into this newly formed relationship with my brother. It's also her young son. If Justin discovers he's not ready to be in it for the long haul, he wouldn't be breaking one heart, he'd be breaking two." Something she would be smart to remember. It was one thing to consider risking her own heart again, but she knew that Lucas would get hurt as well if things didn't work out. Her son admired and looked up to Jackson, even had a special connection with him.

Jackson appeared to take in her words, a slight frown pulling at his mouth. Then he reached into the box and began unwrapping another ornament. "We need to have faith that your brother will handle this budding relationship with Jessica with care. But if it will make you feel any better I'll have a talk with him about it."

She moved to hang another ornament from the tree. "It would. Especially because I know what it's like to be a single mother with a son who's hurting emotionally."

"Justin would never hurt Jessica intentionally. But we men don't always handle situations the way we should have," he said, making Lainie wonder if he was referring to that night so long ago. "One thing I do know for sure is that if your brother does, however unintentionally, hurt Jessica in any way, he'll have to deal with Hannah and Garrett, who have pretty much made Jessica and Dustin a part of their family."

"She's blessed to have such good friends," she said as she stepped around to the far side of the tree with another ornament. "Life isn't easy to maneuver on one's own."

Jackson looked her way. "I know things haven't been easy for you since Will died, but I hope you know that you're not alone anymore."

She met his gaze, the kindness in his green eyes melting her heart. "Thank you for saying that."

"It's not just words, Lainie," he told her. "We're all here for you, your family, my family…me. Especially me." He bent to plug the lights into the wall plug. The tree flickered to life, its twinkling lights dancing at random. With a quick adjustment, Jackson had them glowing a solid white. "Now all we need is the star."

The heirloom Lainie held in her hands had been in the family for generations and had been left at the house when their parents moved out. Their mother had chosen to take with them the angel topper their father had given her for Christmas ten years before, instead, saying it had sentimental meaning to her.

"Would you like me to get a chair from the kitchen for you to stand on?" Jackson said, pulling her from her thoughts. "Or would you rather I grab you a ladder from the garage?"

She held the precious antique glass star out to him with a smile. "No need. I think you're tall enough to place the star atop the tree."

"Me?"

"Yes, you," she told him. "I wouldn't have a tree to put up if it weren't for you."

"Maybe you should leave it for Justin or Lucas to put on."

"Neither of them has any interest in holiday decorations," she said, wishing it were otherwise. Seeing his hesitation, she said, "It would mean a lot to me if you were to place the star."

He glanced down at the precious family heirloom she held in her outstretched hands and then back up at

Lainie, tenderness filling his eyes. "I would be honored."

She stood watching as Jackson Wade slid her family's star down over the top branch, carefully adjusting it until it stood perfectly straight. Then he stepped back to join her, the two of them admiring their handiwork together.

"Perfect," she said with a sigh.

"Perfect," he agreed.

The tree hadn't been the only thing she'd been referring to, however. It had been the time they'd spent together that afternoon. The ease with which they'd fallen back into their long-ago friendship. The comfort she found in spending time with Jackson. She sent a silent prayer of thanks to the Lord for bringing Jackson back into her life again, and for giving her the strength and ability to forgive him for breaking her heart the way he had. Rebuilding their friendship had helped to heal a large part of her. Now she prayed for the strength to hold on to that friendship without pressing him for more. Because *more* wasn't something she was prepared to offer to anyone. Especially Jackson Wade.

Chapter Seven

Seeing the barn door ajar, Lainie let her son race on ahead to Jackson's parents' house, while she was drawn in a different direction. Tucking her hands into the fleece-lined pockets of her winter coat, she crossed the sun-warmed yard, a smile already on her face at the thought of seeing Jackson. Even for a few moments. She wondered if he felt the same way, considering how close he'd come to kissing her just a couple of days before.

Lainie stepped into the oversize building and caught sight of Jackson's youngest brother across the way, busily at work inside one of the empty horse stalls. "Morning, Tucker," she greeted with a smile.

He straightened, glancing her way. "Lainie," he replied with a wave of greeting and then a troubled expression moved over his face. "Tell me you didn't walk here."

"I didn't," she assured him. "Not that I haven't walked that distance before. Even in winter. However, Justin dropped Lucas and me off on his way to work. I wanted to save Autumn a trip out to my brother's place to get us." She hoped to buy a car of her own someday and continue working on getting comfortable behind the wheel of a vehicle. It was just a little too soon for that big of a commitment. She planned to take baby steps. But she was determined to make it happen.

The Wades were going to watch the children while she, Autumn, Hannah and Jessica drove into town to pick up baskets various businesses had offered to donate for their cause after they'd had gone around town posting flyers the week before.

"I hear you ladies are heading out to do a gift basket collection run," he said.

"We are," she replied, her gaze searching for Jackson. "Is your brother around?"

"I take it you're not referring to Garrett," he answered with a teasing grin, his older brother having returned from the NFR in Vegas a few days earlier.

Her cheeks warmed. "No."

"Didn't think so," he said with a knowing grin. "Jackson isn't back yet. He ran into town to the post office to mail out a couple of contracts. Something I can help you with?"

Lainie shook her head. "No. I just wanted to say hi." Hearing herself, she felt a little foolish hunting Jackson down just to say hello to him.

Tucker rested the shovel handle against the barn wall and then stepped over to stand at the closed gate, resting his folded arms atop it. "It's good to see you and my brother on speaking terms again."

She lowered her gaze. "It shouldn't have gone on so long."

He gave his head a slow shake. "Nope. Not when the two of you had feelings for each other."

Her head snapped up. "Jackson didn't have feelings for me. He's my brother's best friend. He was mine, too, back then. My problem was wanting more than he was prepared to give me. Not when the rodeo life had such a hold on his heart."

"You really think that was all there was to it?" he asked in surprise.

"He told me so," she countered, feeling defensive. Tucker hadn't been there. She had.

"Maybe he felt it best at the time to let you go on believing that," he muttered as he reached up to pluck a piece of straw from his flannel work shirt.

"I don't understand," she told him, puzzled.

"I've already said more than I should have," he admitted with a sigh. "If you want the full truth, you'll need to ask my brother. And while you're at it, you might consider telling him the truth about Vegas as well. Openness goes both ways."

Guilt pinched in her chest. "I'm not sure what you're referring to," she said, unable to look him in the eye. Jackson must have told his brothers about her poorly timed phone call.

"I'm referring to the visit you paid to the hospital in Las Vegas after Jackson's accident."

A small gasp left her lips.

"I was there that day," he went on. "I'd left Jackson's room to make a few phone calls. When I was done, I stepped from the waiting area down the hall from Jackson's room just in time to see you walk up to the door of his private room. You stood there staring at it for a very long while, as if trying to gather your thoughts before going in. I nearly called out to you, and then thought better of it. I know how much my brother had been missing you and the close relationship the two of you had formed over the years. I also knew how much your being there would've meant to him. I prayed it would help give Jackson the push he needed on his road to recovery, because he was in a bad place, both physically and emotionally."

"It tore me up when Justin called to tell me what had happened to Jackson," she said. She hadn't watched the one televised rodeo he was competing in, but maybe it was a blessing. Just hearing about what had happened had been devastating enough. The next thing Lainie knew she was on a plane bound for Vegas, thanking the Lord for not taking Jackson away far too soon from those who loved him, and praying for Him to ease Jackson's pain.

Tucker nodded. "It tore all of us up. We never thought we'd be waiting to see if my brother, one of the best bull riders on the circuit, was going to survive the battering he'd taken from one of those bulls. How Jackson ever let that bull get the better of him, we have no idea." He stood shaking his head in wonder, even now, years later. "It was as if he'd never gotten his head into the ride."

Because I had taken his head out of the ride, Lainie thought sorrowfully.

Tucker went on, "I fully expected to see you step into that room. Instead, you leaned your head against the open door and closed your eyes. Before I could decide whether to hold back, or to go see if you needed me to go in with you to see Jackson, you had stepped away, running off down the hospital corridor like someone had lit a fire to your heels."

Lainie pressed a hand to her mouth, unable to speak.

The guilt she'd felt that day when she'd told her fiancé she had to leave town for a couple of days to visit a close family friend who had been injured badly came rushing back. It hadn't been a lie. Jackson *was* a close family friend, but he was so much more than that to her.

"He knew I was there?" she said fretfully, the words an anxious whisper.

"I never told him," Tucker replied with a frown. "Figured if you had wanted him to know you were there, you would have gone in to see him."

"Thank you," she breathed.

Tucker looked down at her, his expression contemplative. "Why didn't you go in to see him that day, Lainie? After coming all the way from California to do so."

"I couldn't," she said sadly. As much as she had wanted to be by his side until she knew he would be okay, she didn't deserve to be. Not only because she was engaged to another man—one she cared deeply about—but because she blamed herself for his being there. If only she hadn't called him with her news that day…but she hadn't known he was preparing to ride in the rodeo finals.

"I know it would have been hard for you to see him that way, all bruised and broken, but I truly believe your being there would have made a big difference in Jackson's will to come back from such a devastating injury."

"I had no right to be there," she said with a choked sob. "I was engaged to another man, to Will. I had no right to be there. No right to still have feelings for Jackson when I loved another. And I did love my husband, Tucker. Truly I did."

His expression softened. "I know you did, Lainie. Sometimes first loves never quite leave our hearts completely. Even when they ought to."

"Blue's mother?"

"Yes," he replied. "She gave me one of the biggest blessings in my life—my daughter. And for that I will always hold a special place in my heart for her. But there's only one woman who has ever made me feel whole, like everything in my life is finally set to rights, and that's Autumn. Love is just different with her. Better. Brighter." He rolled his eyes. "Will you listen to me? Here I go, getting all mushy like some lovesick fool. I swear marriage and babies turn men into walking, talking, cowboy-hat-wearing marshmallows."

She felt a hint of a smile return to her face. "You don't sound like a fool at all. You sound like a man truly in love."

"I am that," he agreed. "Long story short, the heart is a wondrous organ, fully capable of loving more than one person in many different ways. A fortunate thing for me, considering how large the Wade family is becoming."

As wondrous as the heart might be, it was an unruly organ. The more she tried to convince her heart that she was past her love for Jackson, the more it set out to prove her wrong. "I think a part of me will always love your brother," she admitted with a soft sigh. "But we're at different places in our lives now. I'm raising a child. He's running a business."

"That doesn't mean the two can't connect," he muttered as he studied her reaction to his words.

"I appreciate what you're trying to do," she told him, "but Jackson and I are what we were always meant to be—friends. Besides, Lucas is just getting settled into his new life. I need to focus on him, and not my own wants and needs right now." She glanced at her watch, noting the time. "I need to get going. Everyone will probably be wondering where I am."

He nodded in understanding. "Think about what I said. You know what they say about the truth setting you free."

"I will," she replied. "Thank you for not saying anything to Jackson about Vegas. And thank you for the talk."

"Anytime," he said, turning to grab the shovel he'd set aside. "You girls have fun."

"With those three, I have no doubt we will." Turning, she walked out of the barn, their conversation playing over and over in her mind.

Jackson waited until Lainie had gone into the main house before stepping out from behind the tractor parked next to the barn. He hadn't meant to eavesdrop on her conversation, but when he'd overheard Tucker telling her that he'd seen her at the rehabilitation facility in Vegas, he couldn't bring himself to take another step, forward or backward. He stood frozen in place, listening to the scene his brother was describing and then Lainie's heart-tugging response. He had hurt her to the point she couldn't bear to be around him for years afterward, yet she had flown to Las Vegas to see him when she'd learned of his injury. A part of her still loved him now. His heart had soaked up her admission, giving him all the more reason to hope for more than friendship between them.

He glanced down at his bad leg; covered in denim, it

looked like any other man's. Underneath his jeans was a badly scarred thigh and hip, plates, rods and screws now holding them together. The repairs allowed him to ride again, but a bronc, and definitely not any more bulls. Even now, years later, he still experienced some discomfort when riding his horse. But he hadn't let that keep him from doing it altogether—not when horses were such a huge part of his life.

Still trying to wrap his head around what he'd overheard, Jackson stepped into the barn.

Tucker glanced up when Jackson entered the barn, greeting his brother with a smile. "You just missed Lainie."

"I know."

"Oh, you ran into her outside," Tucker said in understanding as he moved to let himself out of the stall he'd been mucking out.

"Actually, I made sure we didn't run into each other."

His brother paused to look his way, his hand stilled on the gate he'd been latching shut. "I was under the understanding the two of you had worked things out."

"We have," Jackson replied. "At least we're working on it."

"Then why are you suddenly avoiding her?"

"Because I'm still trying to process what I just overheard."

Tucker released the gate and turned to face him, a hint of worry in his expression. "Overheard?"

"How could you have kept something like this from me?" Jackson demanded. "You've known all these years that Lainie had come to Vegas after my accident, yet you've never said a word about it to me. Not one word."

"I thought Mom taught you better than to eavesdrop on others' conversations," his brother replied without apology.

"I wasn't," Jackson began in his own defense, and then wondered why he felt the need to defend what he had done. Tucker was the one who should have been explaining his actions, keeping the truth from his own brother. If Jackson had known about Lainie's hospital visit in Vegas, it might very well have changed the direction of his life. "I didn't mean to eavesdrop," he went on. "I was on my way into the barn when I heard you telling Lainie you had seen her at the hospital in Vegas. I was trying to make sense of what I was hearing, because as far as I knew she'd never been there. And then Lainie admitted to you that she still loved me. I didn't think it was the best time to announce my arrival, so I stood outside waiting for the conversation to end, but it didn't." He met his brother's gaze and said, as if still trying to digest the information, "She came to Vegas." The very knowledge of it made his heart stir.

Tucker let out a heavy sigh. "She did."

"Why would you keep something like that from me?" he asked in frustration. If he had known, maybe, just maybe, he could have set things right with Lainie years sooner. He might have ended up being the one to stand waiting for her at the altar, bad leg or not. Lucas might have been *his* son. Funny how he'd never thought about having a family, a son to call his own, until Lainie had come home. And now it seemed to fill his thoughts constantly.

Tucker crossed the room to put the shovel away.

"If you overheard, then you know why I never mentioned it."

"Your first loyalty should have been to me, not Lainie."

His brother spun on booted heel to face him, his expression darkening. "In case you've forgotten, you nearly lost your life the night Lucky Shamrock trampled you into the floor of that Vegas arena. Garrett and I thought you were dead when we saw you lying there lifeless in the dirt," he said, his voice thick with emotion.

A knot formed in Jackson's throat when he heard the pain behind the anger in those words. "I haven't forgotten anything," he told him. "How can I, when I'm forced to live with a constant reminder of that fall? And I was lifeless because I'd been knocked unconscious."

"That bull kicked you around like you weighed no more than Blue's precious little rag doll. I don't think I'd ever prayed harder in my life than I did at that moment. But since I was preaching to Lainie about the truth setting you free, I'll answer your question. I never said anything to you about her being there, not only because if she had wanted you to know she would have gone into your room that day, but because I wasn't about to lose you."

Jackson's brows drew together. "What does that have to do with your losing me?"

His brother peeled off his work gloves. "Everything. You were in bad enough shape to the point that it was touch and go for a while. If Lainie had gone in to see you that day, it might have given you the spark you needed to get through things. But to tell you she had come to Vegas and then left without speaking to you would have only dragged you down further mentally. Maybe even physically. Right or wrong, I did what I thought was best at the time, and I'd do it all over again if the situation was the same. And if you're going to be mad at anyone, be mad at me. Garrett doesn't know about Lainie's showing up in Vegas either."

No doubt because Garrett hadn't been there at the hospital with Tucker. He'd been waiting in the parking lot outside, exchanging fretful phone calls with Tucker. Garrett hadn't been able to step foot inside any hospital since losing his high school sweetheart after a long, hard battle with leukemia. It wasn't until he'd rescued Hannah from the flood and she'd gone into labor that he'd forced himself to pass through the same hospital doors he'd last gone through to say goodbye to his young sweetheart.

Letting go of his anger and that feeling of having been betrayed, which he knew Tucker would never truly do, Jackson met his brother's gaze. "Put that way, I can understand why you handled things the way you did. I just wish I had known." He glanced toward the door.

"She still loves you."

His attention slid back to Tucker and a slow smile spread across his face. "That's what I'm counting on."

"Thank you again for including me in your gift basket drive," Lainie said as she and the other women climbed into Hannah's brand-new minivan.

"Yes, thank you," Jessica said with a nod. "I've been so excited for this and the feeling it brings, knowing that I'm going to be helping others in need. Especially, during the holidays when a family's financial strain weighs so much more heavily on them. As someone who was once a young, single mother without a career to fall back on, I know firsthand what it feels like to struggle to make ends meet," she stated. They had done so before her husband's life insurance and other monies had been released to her after his passing. Her husband had been good with finances, and while they weren't wealthy now, they were able to live a comfortable life.

Lainie couldn't imagine what it would have been like to raise a child in that situation. Will had always had a secure job with a generous income. They'd never had to struggle to put food on the table. She had to admire Jessica for surviving her hardships and persevering in spite of them and to come out of it all such a positive, happy person. It was no wonder Justin was so taken with her.

"Hannah and I are thrilled to have you both be a part of this," Autumn said as she settled into the front passenger seat, clutching her copy of the list of businesses they were to pick baskets up from.

Hannah settled behind the wheel. "And it will help us get all the baskets collected far quicker than it would have if it were just Autumn and I."

As Lainie took a seat behind Autumn and reached for her seat belt, she caught sight of Jackson's truck and her heart gave a foolish little lurch. Why couldn't she put her thoughts of him back into the friend zone where they had once been? Maybe because of the kiss they'd almost shared when they were putting up the Christmas tree.

"Would you like to go say hello before we leave?"

She turned to find all three women watching her, smiles on their faces. She didn't have to ask who Hannah was referring to. She knew. "I'll see Jackson when we get back. He's going to be giving Lucas more riding lessons today and then take us home."

"Garrett's really happy to see the two of you spending so much time together," Hannah said as they pulled away from Emma and Grady's place.

"I think Emma's pretty happy about it, too," Autumn chimed in.

Just what she was afraid of. "Don't read anything more than friendship into it," Lainie told them. "I'm not looking for a relationship. I have my son to think of."

"Exactly why you should keep the option open," Autumn told her. "He's so good with Lucas. And I've seen the smile that comes to your face every time Jackson looks your way."

"Jackson has been so good to us, but I can assure you nothing is going to come of the time we spend together other than friendship," she told them.

"I thought that, too," Jessica mumbled. "And then your brother came into my life."

Lainie's head snapped around, her gaze focusing on the smiling young woman beside her. "Things are getting serious with my brother?"

"We're not looking to walk down the aisle or anything," she replied. "But he's a very special man. And my son likes him, which was the most important factor in my decision as to whether or not to see Justin again."

"My brother is a good man," Lainie acknowledged without hesitation. "And he's so good with Lucas."

"With Blue, too," Autumn interjected. "But then I think it's more his shiny sheriff's star badge that draws her to him."

"Same here," Jessica said, a soft giggle following.

Lainie debated expressing her concerns but decided she should for Dustin's sake. "My brother can be a workaholic at times. He's very committed to his job."

"That's what I admire about him," Jessica said almost dreamily. "I understand that type of commitment. I'm the same way with my nursing career and wanting to help others. Sometimes, actually most of the time, at the cost of our own personal lives. It's hard to date someone who doesn't appreciate the changing shifts and sometimes long hours. But your brother understands that."

"A match made in Heaven," Hannah said with a dramatic sigh.

"Not too many good ones left out there," Autumn agreed. "Especially since Hannah and I managed to snag two of the best around."

"There is one Wade brother left, however," Hannah hinted, her gaze shifting in Lainie's direction.

Lainie's heart was telling her to grab on to Jackson before some other woman did. But it had led her astray once before where he was concerned. Lainie was torn between listening to her heart or her head when it came to her feelings for Jackson. "Jackson's my brother's best friend," she countered, as if that fact automatically placed him out of the running for her affection.

Hannah and Autumn exchanged knowing glances, before Autumn said, "Okay, we'll stop pushing. Just know that we wouldn't have any objection to having you and Lucas join our ever-growing family."

Oh, how she longed for that to be what her future held. "It would be nice to have sisters," she replied. "But," she added, "I'm going to have to settle for dear friends instead, Jessica included."

"Unless she marries Justin," Autumn said in a sing-song voice that had Jessica blushing.

"You girls have marriage on the brain," Jessica replied with a smile and a shake of her head.

Jackson is a loving man, Lainie thought. To his family, to his horses, to the Lord. It was her he hadn't been able to love. At least, not in the way she'd wanted him to.

The women chattered on about anything and everything, from jobs to babies, to the town's upcoming Christmas social and dance that was fast approaching. While Lainie sat in contemplative silence, her thoughts playing over the conversation she'd had with Tucker in the barn. What was it that Jackson hadn't been completely open with her about?

"Here we are," Hannah announced as she pulled into a parking space in front of Abby's, the local doughnut and coffee shop.

Lainie got out and grabbed her purse. Tucked inside was the folded sheet of holly-trimmed stationery containing divvied-up lists of the businesses that had agreed to donate.

"I'll leave the van unlocked," Hannah announced as she shoved her car keys into the pocket of her coat. "That way you will be able to drop off baskets as needed. Some might be heavier than others. We can meet back here in…let's say forty-five minutes. If there are any baskets left at that point to be collected, we can finish those up together."

"Sounds like a good plan to me," Hannah said, unfolding her list.

"Aren't you worried someone might take the baskets we'll be leaving in the van?" Jessica asked worriedly.

"That's not really an issue here in Bent Creek," Lainie told her, happy that she once again lived in a place where people didn't fear leaving doors unlocked. Then she caught sight of her brother watching them from the front window of his office and added with a grin, "Besides, I don't think anyone would have the nerve to make off with our baskets with the town sheriff looking on."

Jessica turned, her gaze moving to the old redbrick building across the street.

Lainie's brother raised his coffee cup in acknowledgment of their presence there in town and offered up a wide grin. One of those lovesick puppy kind of grins. Then he lifted his other hand to reveal a large, bow-topped basket of goodies.

Justin was beyond smitten, Lainie thought as she watched the widening smiles he exchanged with Jessica. A part of her wished Jackson would woo her that way. A very big part of her, if she were being honest with herself.

Lainie stopped by the hardware store, where Mr. Randall handed over an open toolbox filled with various tools. A hammer, a set of screwdrivers, a tape measure and a flashlight to name a few of the items Lainie could make out through the cellophane wrapping that covered the sturdy metal box.

"It's not much," he said, eyeing the ribbon-adorned package.

"Oh no, it's perfect," she told him. "And so very useful. I especially like the red and green ribbons hanging down from this beautiful bow."

Her words brought a smile to his weathered face. "My wife took a bow-making class in preparation for

Christmas and she's been itching to put her newfound skill to use, as we haven't done our own holiday shopping for each other yet."

"Well, please tell her that her bow and ribbons are beyond perfect. And thank you for contributing."

"It was my pleasure. And I have to say it's good to have you back home where you belong."

"It's good to be home," she said, meaning it with all her heart. This town was where she belonged.

Lainie carried the wrapped toolbox to the van and then made her way to Sandy's Candies, the next business on her list. The sweet aroma of all the confections made in the back room swarmed her senses the moment she stepped into the store. Warm chocolate with a hint of peppermint drew her over to one of the glass display cabinets where the seasonal Christmas treats were kept.

"Can I help you?"

Turning, Lainie caught sight of Sandy Belmont standing in the back doorway, a tray of just-made confections in her plastic-glove-covered hands. "Hello."

The woman's welcoming smile faltered for just a brief moment, but it was long enough for Lainie to wonder at the cause. "Hello, Lainie," she said, moving to stand behind the cabinet of sweets Lainie had been admiring. "I heard through the local grapevine that you had moved home."

She nodded. "I did. That is, we did. My son, Lucas, and I."

The other woman busied herself with placing the peppermint-candy-sprinkled chocolate squares, one by one, from the tray to one of the holiday platters inside the display case. "Rumor has it you and Jackson have been spending a lot of time together."

Lainie's gaze lifted from the selection of candies in front of her to settle on the other woman's pinched mouth as she busied herself with refilling the display case. "He's been giving my son riding lessons," she said, feeling the need to leave it at that. Sandy, who had graduated with Jackson and Justin, had once been head over heels for Jackson. But that had been back in their sophomore or junior year, and they'd only gone out a few times. Surely, she didn't still have a thing for Jackson after all these years. The thought had no sooner formed in her mind when Lainie realized *she* still had feelings for Jackson after all these years. Why couldn't Sandy still harbor some as well? The possibility didn't sit well with her. Not at all. It killed her to think about Jackson with Sandy, or any other woman. But she had no claim to his heart. "He's been a good friend," Lainie explained simply.

"I wouldn't set my cap for him if I were you," the other woman muttered as she straightened, the now-empty tray in her hands. "Or you'll learn the hard way that Jackson Wade is not the marrying type."

Apparently, her suspicions about Sandy's lingering feelings for Jackson were on target. Had there been more between them than what Lainie knew about from high school? Justin had never mentioned Jackson and Sandy rekindling their old high school relationship. But then Lainie had cut Jackson out of her life when she'd gone off to college. It was possible her brother hadn't said anything, because he assumed Lainie wouldn't care what Jackson Wade was up to.

"Thank you for the advice," Lainie answered with what she hoped was a pleasant smile. She knew what it felt like to be rejected by Jackson and how hard it was to get over him. "My main focus is on my son right now and rebuilding our lives here in Bent Creek. I'm sure you've heard through the 'local grapevine' that I'm a widow now."

Sandy looked shamed by the reminder. "I did. And I'm sorry if I came across as insensitive. I'm not even sure why I felt the need to warn you off Jackson. It's not as if he and I are an item. I just find myself thinking about how things used to be sometimes when he stops by to buy candy for his niece. Only he hasn't been around since you've come home, so I thought…" She shook her head. "Never mind my foolish thoughts. What can I get for you today? The milk chocolate sea salt caramels are really good. So are the assorted holiday truffles."

"They both sound wonderful," Lainie told her. She knew all too well about recalling how things used to be. "How about a half dozen of the sea salt caramels? And can I get two of the chocolate-covered pretzel rods with the red and green sprinkles?"

"Sure thing." Sandy hurried to bag up the order and then carried it over to the cash register to ring it up. "Is there anything else I can get for you?"

How had she almost forgotten her reason for being there? "I'm supposed to be picking up a basket for the church's holiday basket drive."

"Oh, of course," Sandy replied in a fluster. "I have it right here." She turned to a counter and lifted a large red, cellophane-wrapped wicker basket, which she handed over to Lainie. Inside was an assortment of sugary treats, as well as a plush red throw sporting a tiny white snowflake design, four coffee mugs, a tin of hot chocolate and a book of inspirational short stories.

"Thank you for donating," Lainie said. "I know this basket of goodies will mean a lot to some family."

"You're welcome," Sandy said as she checked Lainie out. "I hope they make this an annual event. It felt good putting this basket together, knowing that it would help make some family's Christmas a little more special."

"I hope so, too." Basket and purchases in hand, Lainie left the store and headed back down the sidewalk to drop off her basket and her bag of sweets. Her thoughts went back to her conversation with Sandy, and then to the one she'd had in the car with Autumn, Hannah and Jessica. It would be so easy to give in and allow her heart to have its way where Jackson Wade was concerned. Everyone else already had it in their minds that there was something going on between them anyway. If only life were that simple.

"He's so good," a familiar female voice exclaimed from behind Jackson.

He glanced back over his shoulder, grinning at the sight of Lainie watching her son ride Tumbleweed around the arena in awe. Perfectly understandable, considering the control Lucas had over his mount as it trotted in wide circles around Jackson. "Yep. He's a natural. Must be genetic."

Lainie let herself into the small indoor ring, closing the gate behind her. Then she moved to join Jackson, who stood watching over on the horse. "I'd say it's more due to the fact that my son is being taught by one of the best."

Jackson snorted. "You trying to sweeten me up for some reason?"

"Nope," she said with a smile. "Just giving credit where credit is due. Now, if I were trying to sweeten you up…" Lainie held a chocolate-covered pretzel rod out to him.

"What's this?" he said with a chuckle.

"I know you Wade boys have a thing for sugary treats. This is my way of saying thank you for all you've done. Even if it's not nearly enough to express the gratitude I feel."

"It's more than enough," he countered with a grin as he accepted the thoughtful gift. Bringing it to his mouth, he took a bite and then moaned. "Mmm…this is good. You make them?"

"I'd like to take credit for them, but no," she answered. "I bought them at Sandy's Candies when I stopped by to pick up the basket today that she made for the basket drive. I brought one for Lucas, too, but I can see he's a little too busy for a snack right now."

"We were just finishing up," he told her and then looked toward her son, who was trotting around the far side of the ring. "Lucas," he called out, drawing her son's attention. "A few more rounds and we'll call it a day. Your mom's here."

The second Lucas spotted Lainie, his easygoing smile faded and a tension that hadn't been there before worked its way into the boy's shoulders. Jackson had no doubt Lainie had noticed as well, but she hadn't let the less-than-enthusiastic greeting put her off. Instead, she smiled even brighter.

"You're doing so well," she called out to her son. "Your father would have been so proud of you."

Lucas rode over to the mounting block and brought the horse to a stop. "I'm done," he muttered.

Jackson exchanged a quick glance with Lainie before walking over to place the block next to the horse. Lucas wasted no time in dismounting and then, leaving the horse to Jackson, made his way out of the arena.

"Lucas," Jackson called after him, bringing the boy's steps to a halt.

Her son glanced back over his shoulder.

"Next week we're going to work on your tending to your mount after you're done with your ride, something every cowboy knows how to do."

"Yes, sir," he replied, and then started on his way again.

"I brought you a treat," Lainie said as her son swept past her.

"I don't want anything from you," he called back before breaking into a run.

The stricken look on Lainie's face tugged at Jackson's heart. "Lainie…"

She held up a hand. "Don't say it, Jackson. I don't want your pity," she told him, her bottom lip quivering slightly as if she were fighting to keep control of her emotions.

"His behaving that way is not all right, Lainie," he told her. "He needs to know that."

"He's hurting," she replied, her gaze fixed in the direction her son had run off. "Lucas is already having a hard time where the holiday is concerned without my having brought up his father."

He secured the horse and walked over to where she stood, looking so broken despite her attempt to appear otherwise, and drew her into his comforting arms. "It will get better," he told her. "I promise you." And he would do everything in his power to make it be so.

Chapter Eight

"Jackson?" Lainie said in surprise when she opened the door to her brother's house to find the handsome cowboy standing there.

"Morning," he greeted with his usual warm smile. "Or maybe I should say afternoon, since it's nearly that."

"What are you doing here?"

One lone brow lifted. "Same thing I'm always doing when I stop by. Checking on you and Lucas."

"But I thought Justin called you yesterday to let you off the hook."

"He did, and for the record, I didn't consider myself on the hook."

Lainie lifted a brow in a challenging gesture.

"Okay," he said with a grin, "maybe in the very beginning."

She returned his smile. "Well, you don't have to check up on us anymore," she said, trying not to let her true emotions show at the prospect of his stepping away from the obligation he'd been honor bound to fulfill to her brother. "Now that Sam is sharing shifts with my brother and Deputy Vance, Justin says he'll have more time to spend with us."

"Maybe I don't want to stop watching over you and Lucas," Jackson said, meeting her gaze. "As a matter of fact, work shifts won't be the only thing your brother is going to be sharing."

"No?" she replied, her heartbeat quickening.

"No," he said determinedly. "I intend to be a part of your and your son's lives. Not because of some promise I made, but because I want to be. That is if you want me to be a part of it."

Joy filled her. "Of course I do."

"I know there was a time when you felt differently..." he began.

"I was wrong to shut you out the way I did," she told him. "If I could change the past, I would." She thought of her precious son, and added, "Maybe not all of it. Lucas is my biggest blessing."

"Speaking of Lucas," he said. "How are things between the two of you?"

"Not as good as I'd like them to be, but we're working on it. We had a talk after we got home from his riding lessons yesterday. I made it clear that I love him and know that he's hurting, but that his behavior in the barn was unacceptable. He apologized, so that's something."

"Glad to hear it," he said with a nod. His gaze moved past her. "Speaking of Lucas, I seem to recall it's his birthday today."

"It is." She stepped aside, motioning him into the house.

"You two have plans?" he asked as he joined her in the entryway.

She nodded. "We're having a birthday dinner here

tonight. My parents are coming over. So is Hannah and Dustin. You, too, I hope, if you're free. I know this is last minute, but Justin just suggested it this morning and Lucas wanted to be the one to invite you."

"I'd be honored to be a part of your son's big day," he told her. "Do you have a lot to do to prepare for Lucas's party tonight or do you think you and Lucas could spare an hour or so to take a ride with me?"

She glanced back at the clock on the entry wall and then to Jackson. "Justin is bringing home pizza and chips, so I won't have to cook, and I baked Lucas's cake this morning."

"So your answer is yes?"

"Lucas!" Lainie called out with a smile. "Get your coat. Jackson is taking us for a drive."

His lone-dimpled grin widened.

Her son came running down the stairs. "Mr. Wade!"

"Birthday boy!" he greeted in response.

If only her son's face lit up that way when he saw her. But he was happy on this very special day and that was all that mattered. Grabbing her coat from the hall tree, she hurried to slip it on. "Where are we going?" she asked as she turned to face Jackson.

"To my place," he answered as he opened the door. "So I can give Lucas his birthday present."

"You got me a present?" her son said as he stepped past Jackson and out onto the porch.

"I did," he said with a nod.

"But I didn't get to invite you to my party yet," Lucas told him with a troubled frown.

"You're having a party?" Jackson said, feigning surprise as he cast a quick glance at Lainie.

"We are," her son replied as they made their way

toward Jackson's truck. "And you're invited. Can you come? We're having pizza."

"It's your birthday. I wouldn't miss it for the world," Jackson told him as he led them to his truck. "Just tell me what time I need to be here."

Lucas looked to Lainie. "What time is my party?"

"Six o'clock."

"I'll be there," Jackson said as he reached out to open the rear passenger door for Lucas. "But I'm going to give you your present now. If that's okay."

Lainie glanced back to see her child nodding excitedly. Laughing softly, she said, "I think that's a yes."

Jackson helped her up into the truck and then walked around to the driver's side. "Buckle up," he said as he did so himself.

"Already done," Lainie assured him as she settled back in her seat.

They were pulling up to Jackson's place in no time at all, but then he did live right next door to her brother.

Lucas started for the house, making Lainie grin knowingly. Jackson stopped them. "Your present isn't in the house. It's in the barn."

"The barn?" Lucas said in confusion.

"Too big to keep in my house," Jackson told him as he led them across the yard.

Jackson had called to ask her permission to give Lucas the gift he had in mind. A gift her son was sure to love. The thought had barely settled in her mind when they stepped into the barn and she saw them. Not one, but two long faces looking back at her from above the adjacent stall gates. The smaller of the two bedecked in a bright red bow.

"Happy birthday, Lucas," he said with a wide grin.

The horses nickered in greeting as Jackson, Lainie and Lucas moved toward them.

"The one with the fancy ribbon tied to its mane is yours, Lucas. That is, if you want him."

"Mine?"

"Yep. His name is Cody," Jackson said. "He's named after Buffalo Bill Cody."

"I love him!" her son exclaimed.

Jackson chuckled. "I'll take that as a yes, that you want him."

Her son nodded eagerly.

"We'll keep him here until you've learned the basics of riding and caring for a horse of your own."

"What do you tell Jackson?" Lainie prompted with a smile.

"Thanks!"

"You're welcome. Happy birthday."

As Lucas stood admiring his new gift, Jackson inclined his head for Lainie to step over to the adjoining stall. "This is Annie." He looked to Lainie. "She's yours if you want her."

"Jackson, I told you giving Lucas a horse was too much, even though you convinced me to let you do so. But this is truly too much."

"Lainie, I've got more than enough horses to call my own," he explained. "And these two Paints are sweet natured and used to being ridden."

"Jackson, I can't. It's Lucas's birthday, not mine," she said.

"Maybe so, but this is for all those birthdays of yours I missed," he replied, his tone tender.

"Jackson," she said again, scarcely able to get the words out. It had been years since she'd ridden, and she'd missed those carefree days. Missed the horse she'd grown up with. The one she'd sold before she went off to college, because Flapjack had deserved to be with someone who took him for rides and loved him as she had always done.

"These two needed to find a new home pretty fast and I thought about you and Lucas. Autumn mentioned that you were looking to buy a place with a barn, so you could get a couple of horses."

"After I *had* a barn," she pointed out as she took in the beautiful Paint, her heart melting.

"I suppose this is what they refer to as putting the horse before the cart. Or barn, as would be the case here."

"Can we keep them?" Lucas said as he moved to stroke the white blaze running down the center of his horse's nose, eliciting even more soft nickers.

Lainie looked to Jackson.

"Before you say anything, know that you are welcome to keep them here for as long as you need to. And they can stay here permanently if something happens and you don't buy a place with a barn. But they will be yours and Lucas's either way, and he can start riding Cody instead for his lessons."

"Mom," her son pleaded anxiously.

"Yes," she said with a soft sigh, her hand coming to her mouth as she fought the rush of emotions moving through her. "We can keep them."

"Yes!" Lucas shrieked, pumping a tiny fist in the air. His action caused the horses to pull back warily. He looked to Jackson with a worried frown. "I forgot to use my quiet voice."

Jackson chuckled. "I think they'll forgive you."

Lucas surprised them both by wrapping his arms around Jackson's waist in a tight bear hug. "This is the best present ever."

A soft gasp caught in Lainie's throat at her son's re-action. She'd known he'd be excited, but it had been so long since she'd seen him display real warmth toward another. Jackson had done even the specialists hadn't been able to do. He'd managed to get past the emotional wall Lucas had built up around himself, one that had begun to seem unbreachable.

Jackson looked to Lainie in panic, as if he feared he'd crossed a line he shouldn't have crossed. That she might resent him for the show of gratitude her son seemed determined to keep from her.

She offered a reassuring smile, wishing she could say more. But she didn't want to do or say anything that would cause Lucas to take a step back when he had just taken such a huge one forward. "A horse does make for a very special gift. Especially for ones in need of a home. Thank you so much for thinking of us."

Relief eased the look of tension on Jackson's face. "It wasn't hard," he admitted, meeting Lainie's gaze. "The two of you are never far from my mind."

Before she could respond, her son released his hold on Jackson to ask, "Can I ride him now?"

Lainie looked over to see Cody once more nudging his nose in Lucas's direction.

"Your mom has a birthday party to prepare for today, and I have some things to see to at the main ranch before the festivities begin," Jackson replied. "How about we all take a short ride around the ranch tomorrow? Get to know your new mounts."

Her son's eyes widened. "Outside?"

"Outside," Jackson confirmed. "You, your mom and me." He looked to Lainie. "That is if it's all right with you. I think he's ready."

Was her son ready to leave the relatively safe confines of the barn's indoor ring? All she could do was trust in Jackson to know if he was or wasn't. He'd been the one working with Lucas. And Jackson Wade was one of the best there was when it came to riding.

"It's been so long since I've ridden," she said. "It sounds like fun. And Lucas can show me what he's learned." Especially since her son hadn't been keen on her watching him during his riding lessons. He said it made him mess up. She'd made certain to give him some breathing room when it came to his lessons.

"Then tomorrow's a go," Jackson said, his grin widening. He turned to Lucas and gave his hair a tousle. "Before I take you two home, would you mind very much if we swung by Tucker's place? I believe Blue has a little special something waiting there for you, too."

Lucas's face lit up even more. "She does?"

"That's so sweet of her," Lainie said. Jackson's family had taken Lucas under its wing. They'd done the same with her as well when she was growing up. Only now that wing included Tucker's and Garrett's wives. Women who were now her friends, offering her the same unconditional love and support the Wades had always shown her.

Her son looked up at the horse Jackson had gifted him with. "I'll be back tomorrow."

Smiling, Lainie reached out to run her hand down the mare's neck. "So will I." It had been so long since she'd gone riding with Jackson. Excitement she hadn't felt for a very long time fluttered in her belly. And once again, Jackson Wade was the reason behind it. His connection with her son drew her to him all the more. He was so good with Lucas, with Blue, even with the babies. She had to wonder if Jackson realized what a good father he would make someday. There was no ignoring the thought that followed: *a good husband as well*. Or the ache that undeniable acknowledgment caused in her heart.

"Happy birthday, dear Lucas. Happy birthday to you!" everyone sang in unison that night at the birthday party.

"Make a wish before you blow out your candles," Lainie told her son as he leaned over the cake she had baked for him.

Her son sat staring at the candles.

"Come on, Lucas," Jessica's son, Dustin, pleaded. "Make a wish. I'm ready for some cake."

"Dustin," Jessica softly scolded, her gaze fixed on Lainie's son, a worried expression on her face.

"I can't," Lucas said, his earlier joy gone. "I'll never get what I really want."

Lainie's heart sank. She knew what her son wanted more than anything—for his father to be back in their lives again. But that wasn't going to happen. Will was gone for good.

"I'd say take a rain check on it." Jackson spoke up from the far end of the kitchen table where they all had gathered. "You might find something later you'd like to wish for."

"Can he do that?" Dustin asked, looking to his mother.

"Sure can," Justin answered. "Unused birthday

wishes are good for a whole year, but you only get one each birthday."

Lainie's mom reached out to pat her grandson's hand. "Just blow your candles out, sweetie, and stick that wish in your back pocket for later."

Heads bobbed in agreement around the table, their understanding where her son was concerned so very touching.

Just when Lainie feared her son was going to jump up from the table and run off, the way he tended to do whenever he was struggling emotionally, Lucas inhaled, leaned forward and proceeded to blow out all eight candles in one try.

Lainie's father gave a low whistle. "Those are some impressive lungs, son."

"He takes after his mother," Justin said with a teasing grin.

Lainie tensed, waiting for her son to reject the notion that he was anything at all like his mother. But to her surprise, he said, "I ride like her, too."

Relief and surprise swept through her at his response. Lainie felt a hand cover hers beneath the table, giving it a supportive squeeze. She offered Jackson a grateful smile, before saying, "Something tells me he's going to be an even better rider than I was at his age." She looked to Lucas. "I can't wait to see you on your new horse."

"Not sure how I'm supposed to compete with a horse," Justin muttered, his grin evidence that he was merely giving Jackson a hard time.

"Blame my brothers," Jackson said with a smile.

"Your brothers?" Lainie queried. "It was their idea for you to get Lucas a horse for his birthday?"

He nodded. "Tucker gave Blue a coloring book of horses. And Garrett gave Hannah's son the old wooden rocking horse he'd had as a boy. I couldn't let them one-up me. I needed to give the best equine gift I could."

"Can't get any better than a real horse," Justin remarked with a chuckle.

Lainie laughed. "You Wade brothers and your competitive nature." Something she was grateful for, if it had played even a small part in Jackson's generous gesture.

"I'd rather have a real one then a wooden one," Lucas said as his grandmother handed him the first slice of birthday cake.

"Me, too," Dustin said, eyeing the slice of cake Lainie's mother was now pushing his way.

"I'll have to keep that in mind," Lainie's brother said with a glance in Jackson's direction.

"Don't even think about it, Justin Dawson," Jessica told him. "I know nothing about taking care of a horse."

"Maybe Mr. Wade could teach us like he's teaching Lucas," Dustin suggested.

"I'd be happy to," Jackson offered.

"I'm pretty good in the saddle as well," Justin said. "If you want riding lessons, I can give them to you."

"You don't have a horse," Lainie pointed out. The hours her brother had put in at work gave him no time to ride, so he'd sold his mount years before.

"I've been thinking about getting myself one again," he replied. "As soon as we're back to a full workforce, I intend to divvy up my workload a little more, which would give me more time for things outside of work. Like riding."

And Jessica, Lainie thought with an inner smile.

She liked the nurse very much and was grateful for the changes she seemed to have brought about in Justin. And her brother wasn't the only one finding happiness. After such a dark time in her life, Jackson had become her light, bringing her more joy than she'd known in a very long time.

"I am so relieved to hear that," Lainie's mother said. "You work yourself to the bone and your father and I are getting too old to have to worry overly about the well-being of our children."

Which was exactly why Lainie had kept her issues with her son from her parents.

"As if that's going to change your worry level over your children," Lainie's father said with a snort. "You live to fuss and worry over your children, grown or not."

She smiled lovingly at her husband of nearly fifty years. "I suppose I do. Just as I worry over you. Speaking of which, I should help you clean up. Your father and I need to be getting home. He's not keen on driving at night anymore."

He nodded. "True. The old eyes aren't what they used to be." Her father looked to the others. "I'm a blessed man to have such a caring woman watching over me."

The eyes might not be, but the heart was, Lainie thought as she listened to her parents exchange of words. The love they still felt for each other was evident in their words, in the tender looks they gave each other, in their actions. Lainie longed to know that same kind of deep, everlasting connection of the heart, something she had almost found with Will. But he'd been taken from her before that bonding that came with time could fully take root. Her thoughts turned to Jackson and she could see, with such clarity, that the boy she'd given her heart to could become the man who could give her that everlasting love.

"No need, Mom," Lainie said. "There's not much to clean up. You and Dad get going. Because you're not the only ones who worry. Just be sure to call me when you get home."

"We will, honey." She stood and moved to the chair Lucas was sitting in, kissing her grandson on the top of his head. "Happy birthday, sweetie."

"Thanks, Grandma," Lainie's son replied, then he looked to his grandfather. "Thanks for the video game."

"You're welcome, son," Lainie's father replied. "Enjoy."

Hugs were exchanged as her parents said goodbye.

"We should get going, too," Jessica said as she walked over to help Lainie with the dishes. "I work the morning shift tomorrow."

"Leave these be," Lainie told her. "There isn't much to wash up. I'll do them after everyone is gone." She had used paper plates to serve the pizza and birthday cake and only had to wash the utensils.

"I'll go grab our coats," Justin said.

"Can I ride with you to take them home?" Lucas asked from where he sat, working on a puzzle with Dustin.

"If it's all right with your mother," her brother told him, looking to Lainie for her decision.

Lucas swung his gaze in her direction, too. "Can I, Mom?"

"Can he?" Dustin asked excitedly. "Then I could show him my room and let him hold Spot."

"You have a puppy?" Lainie asked with a smile.

"Pet lizard," Jessica explained.

"He's a leopard gecko," Dustin clarified with a toothy grin.

"Thus the name Spot," her brother said.

"A gecko," Lainie repeated in surprise, suddenly very thankful that Jackson had gotten her son a horse and not a lizard. She wasn't as comfortable with reptiles as she was with farm animals. She met her son's imploring gaze. "As long as you don't bring a lizard home with you, you can go with Uncle Justin."

"I won't."

"Okay, birthday boy," her brother said. "Go upstairs and grab your coat while I go get ours."

"Come on," Lucas said to Dustin, the two of them racing from the room.

A few minutes later, Lainie and Jackson stood at the edge of the porch waving goodbye as Justin's SUV drove away.

"Well," she said, turning to Jackson, "that went well. Better than expected, honestly. And I owe part of that to you."

"Me?" he said with a chuckle. "What did I do?"

"You know full well what you did," she told him, poking a playful finger into his chest. "Telling my son to save his wish for something he might want later on."

His playful expression grew serious. "I knew what Lucas wanted to wish for and saw it taking him to a place he didn't need to be. So I threw that out. Figured a little gentle redirection of his thoughts couldn't hurt."

"Thank you," she said, looking up at him. "For all you've done for my son, for me, for the horses, for caring," she said, emotion causing her words to catch.

"Having your friendship back means the world to me, Jackson."

"I thank the Lord every night for bringing you back into my life," he admitted. "I've missed you."

"Same here," she said, growing teary-eyed. "Do you have time to talk?" she asked, motioning toward the settee on the porch.

"Always," he said, waiting for her to take a seat before joining her.

She turned, looking up at him. Jackson deserved to know the truth. She just prayed Tucker was right about it setting her free. She'd spent so many years harboring guilt, harboring her unrequited love for Jackson, harboring regret. "I was in Vegas…" she began, praying the admission she was about to make wouldn't ruin all the inroads they had made where their friendship was concerned.

Despite having overheard his brother talking to Lainie that day in the barn, Jackson hadn't expected her to take his advice. Not when she'd kept the truth from him for so long. "You were in Vegas?" he replied, wanting to let her tell her story. He owed her that much.

"The day after your accident," she went on, her hands twisting together nervously on her lap, "I flew to Las Vegas. I needed to see you. Needed to know that you were going to be all right." Tears welled in her beautiful hazel eyes. "Because even if you couldn't love me back, I still loved you. Even when I had no right to, because I was marrying someone else. That's why I left without seeing you. I had to do what was right. I had to let go."

"Lainie," he said, trying to find the words to tell her how her honest admission made him feel.

"You don't have to say anything, Jackson," she told him. "Just hear me out. I've told you before that I blame myself for your accident. I thank the Lord every day you didn't die that night."

"You've been honest with me," he said. "Now it's my turn to tell you the truth. I couldn't tell you that night at the dance when you poured your heart out to me. I loved you." He'd held those words back for so long that finally freeing them from his heart felt as though new life had just been breathed into him.

"What?" she gasped in shock, her wide eyes searching his.

"I know you've heard the saying about if you love someone set them free," he said. "I had to set you free. You had worked so hard for that scholarship. I couldn't in good conscience let you give that up for me, which I knew you would if I had told you how I really felt."

Tears spilled onto her cheeks, shimmering under the faint glow of the porch light above. "You loved me."

He nodded. "I pushed you away emotionally that night, because it was the right thing to do. Even if it tore my heart out to see the hurt I caused you. Foolish young man that I was, I thought time would eventually help to heal the emotional distance you felt the need to put between us. You'd get your degree. And then you'd come home, and we would be free to follow our hearts. I hadn't counted on you shutting me out of your life completely."

"Or marrying someone else," she said sadly.

"Or marrying someone else," he agreed, his words raspy with emotion. He hadn't been prepared for that possibility. Although he should have been. Lainie was a special person with a giving heart.

"Oh, Jackson," she groaned. "If I had known…"

He gave her a tender smile. "Then Lucas wouldn't be a part of your life. I did the right thing. No matter how hard it was to know another man had the love of the only woman to hold my heart."

"Thank you for doing the right thing," she told him. "Because my son means the world to me."

"Thank you for forgiving me and allowing us to rebuild our friendship," he told her, fighting the urge to tell her that he stilled loved her. More now than ever. He wouldn't because, first and foremost, Lainie's focus needed to be on her son, on the new life she was building for her and Lucas there in Bent Creek. And, second, he was no longer the same adventure-seeking young cowboy she had once loved. Time, along with his near-death rodeo accident, had changed him irrevocably. Could Lainie ever bring herself to love the man he had become?

Lainie leaned her head on his shoulder. "I'm so glad we had this talk. My heart feels so much lighter."

He rested his head atop hers. "Me, too, Lainie Girl. Me, too."

"You're the only one who's ever called me that," she murmured against his shirt.

"Among some other names," he told her, needing to lighten things up before he gave in to the urge to kiss her. They both needed to process this new shift in their relationship before taking things any further. "Like Shorty," he went on. "And Pigtails. And—"

Lainie nudged him in the ribs with an elbow. "Those

are ones I can do without being reminded about, thank you very much."

Jackson smiled. This was the closest he'd felt to Lainie in years.

"I'm so glad we moved back," she said with a soft sigh.

"So am I," he told her. "And know that if there's ever anything you need, all you have to do is ask. I'm here for you, Lainie Girl. And for your son."

"There is something…" she said, lifting her head.

"And that something would be?"

"Would you be willing to let me practice driving in your truck again? I can't remain in Bent Creek and not be able to drive. But before I invest in a vehicle of my own, I need to be more comfortable behind the wheel again."

"It'll come," he told her. "And the more you drive, the more at ease you're going to become."

"I pray you're right," she told him. "That day you let me drive your truck I felt more comfortable than I could have ever imagined feeling while sitting behind the wheel again. Maybe I need to look into buying a truck as my next mode of transportation. There's just something about sitting higher up off the ground in a vehicle made for tougher riding conditions that makes me feel safer."

He grinned. "And here I thought we had decided that it was my being there beside you that set you at ease that day."

"No doubt that played into it," she said with a smile.

"Blue is going to be baking cookies with her grandmother tomorrow morning," he told her. "Her favorite pastime. I'm sure Mom won't mind having another helper in the kitchen if you drop Lucas off an hour or so before we set out on our horseback ride around the ranch."

"I'm sure he won't either," she replied with a smile. "Not when cookies of any sort are involved."

"Good. That will give us a chance to take a drive and work on getting you more comfortable behind the wheel. Maybe venture out a little farther away this time around. Like into town."

"Into town," she gasped. "Where there will be other cars?"

"Most roads will have other cars on them," he said calmly.

She frowned. "I know that. I guess I thought I'd just drive up and down your road the first few times. Going into town, where I know there will be traffic, is daunting even to think about."

"Taking back your life, means pushing away those fears that have kept you from doing so," he told her. "Wouldn't it do your heart good to be the one driving to those homes we'll be dropping those gift baskets off to next week? Because I would be more than happy to let you drive when we go."

She appeared to deliberate the possibility for a long moment, and then a small smile drew the corners of her mouth upward. "I can't think of a better reason to work on getting past my fears, than to use that new-found courage to help others in need. And delivering those baskets to those families in need with you by my side will make that day all the more meaningful."

Her words touched him deeply. The great divide that had been between them for so long had shrunk to no more than a miniscule crack now. They were mending emotional fences he'd once thought could never be repaired. And his heart was still invested, despite his determination not to let himself get caught up in the love he'd once felt for Lainie. Still felt for Lainie. And the more time he spent with her—seeing her unfaltering love for her son, joy in helping others, how easily she fit into his family—only made Jackson love her more. Looking out for Lainie and her son no longer felt like an obligation. It felt right, like it was what the good Lord had put him on this earth to do.

Chapter Nine

"Told you he was a natural," Jackson said as he and Lainie rode at an easy pace, just behind Lucas, who had taken the lead on his new mount. His posture was as it should be, his balance right on. Cody was answering the basic physical commands he'd instructed Lucas to use. And the boy was proudly wearing the new blue helmet Jackson had bought for him.

Lainie's smile widened. "It's like he was born in the saddle."

Jackson glanced her way, grinning. "You do notice that he's bound and determined to make us eat his dust. Remind you of anyone?"

She laughed. "I can't help it you and Justin struggled to keep up with me when we were younger. I guess I was just more of a natural than either of you two were."

He chuckled. "Guess so." He couldn't remember the last time he felt this at ease. This happy. Even the slight ache in his bum leg and hip couldn't bring him down. He was doing what he loved with the woman he loved. *Loved.* If it felt this good to think it, he could only imagine how good it was going to feel to say it.

He'd never imagined ever telling any woman after his accident, most especially Lainie, who he'd ended things with years before in such a regrettable way. But the time needed to be right, and that was something he would have plenty of now that Lainie and her son had moved home to Bent Creek.

His gaze drifted to Lainie, recalling the determination with which she took to driving his truck that morning and the smile she'd had on her face when she'd driven all the way down the main street of town and then back again. They had even taken the time to stop by Bent Creek's only car lot, one that carried primarily used vehicles, to look at a few of the trucks. Maybe time didn't just heal all wounds. It healed all fears, too. Because Lainie had put money down on a used, cherry-red, Ford F-150. He had faith that she would be able to drive around without his emotional support someday very soon.

"Annie is such a responsive horse," Lainie said, drawing Jackson from his musings.

"She has a skilled rider," he replied with a grin.

Lainie snorted. "Not sure how skilled I am. It's been years since I've ridden."

"You still have it," he assured her, feeling his grin widen.

His gaze shifted back to Lucas, whose horse was pulling away, having gone from a gentle trot into a canter. "Lucas," Jackson called out, "we're taking the horses on a slow ride today. Nothing faster."

"I'm trying," he called back, his voice showing the slightest amount of panic.

Sensing the boy's fear, Jackson urged his mount to pick up speed until he was riding alongside Lucas.

He had faith in Lucas and his natural instincts when it came to riding, but he wanted to let Lucas know he wasn't alone in this. "Remember what I taught you," he told Lainie's son. "Leaning forward tells the horse you want to pick up speed. This is where you need to sit back in the saddle, keep your heels down and pull back easy on the reins until Cody slows his pace."

Lucas did as instructed, bringing the Paint's gait back down from a fast canter to a walk. "I did it," he gasped.

"You did good, son," Jackson told him. "Now ease up on the reins. Thatta boy."

"Good boy, Cody," Lucas praised with a bright smile.

Lainie caught up to them, mouthing the words *thank you* to Jackson.

He nodded his response, not wanting to make a big fuss over Lucas's momentary loss of control of his mount. The important thing was Lucas's ability to follow direction when faced with an unexpected challenge. Her son was learning and sometimes experience was the biggest lesson of all. Had Lucas not been able to regain control, Jackson would have taken over and slowed the horse for him. He was grateful Lucas had been able to do so on his own, with only a brief reminder of the instructions he'd been given during their many riding lessons together. It had given the boy a sense of pride and accomplishment.

"He's a smart horse," Lainie told her son. Her horse bobbed its head with a whinny. "See, Annie, says so, too."

"Horses can't talk," Lucas countered with a roll of his eyes that looked to Jackson to be more insolent than playful.

"Maybe not the way we do," Jackson said in Lainie's defense as they crossed a wide expanse of pasture. "But they do communicate in their own way. For instance, a snort means there's possible danger. A low nicker means he's glad to see you. A snort can be their way of saying 'what's this?' or simply mean he's bored."

"Wow," Lucas said, his expression now one of genuine awe. "I didn't know they could talk."

"There's a lot you still don't know about horses," Jackson told him. "Things you can learn from your mother, and your uncle, and myself. Any of my family members for that matter," he added. "We've all had years of riding experience."

"Jackson's right," Lainie joined in. "Don't ever be afraid to ask when you're unsure of something. We just want you to be safe. I couldn't bear the thought of anything happening to you," she said, emotion making her voice catch. "I love you."

"You didn't love my dad," Lucas blurted out. "Or he wouldn't be dead."

Lainie's pained gasp echoed in Jackson's ears.

"Lucas," he scolded, beyond disappointed in the boy he'd come to care so much about.

"I'll see you both back at the ranch," Lainie said brokenly.

Before Jackson could respond, she was gone, racing off across the pasture as she had done many times as a young girl. Only this time the hurried ride wasn't one of pleasure or joy. It was one motivated by hurt and the need to distance herself from that pain. Lainie had put up with a lot from her son, and she'd had her reasons for doing so, but this time Lucas had gone too far.

"Pull back on the reins until you bring Cody to a stop," Jackson ground out, praying for patience and calm. "We're going to walk from here."

"But your barn is a long way away," Lucas muttered with a frown.

"A long walk is what you need right now," he told the boy sternly. "It'll give you a chance to think over your actions a moment ago."

Lucas glanced over him, visibly frustrated as he brought his horse to a stop.

Jackson did the same, dismounted and then walked over to Lucas, lifting him down from the Paint with ease while holding both horses in one hand.

"I'm not sorry," Lucas grumbled.

"You should be," Jackson replied. "You just broke the heart of the person who loves you most in the whole world. And it's not the first time you've intentionally set out to hurt your mom. I've seen it and forced myself to let it pass, just as she has, because you've suffered a very painful loss. But you're not the only one hurting. Your mom is, too. And I care far too much about her to just continue to stand by and watch you treat her the way you do." He handed Lucas his reins and then took up his own. "Let's walk."

Grumbling under his breath, Lucas set out on foot across the pasture, leading his horse behind him.

Jackson fixed his gaze on the land ahead of him. Lord help him, because giving tough love hurt his heart. He just prayed it was the right thing to do, because his experience in dealing with troubled children was nonexistent.

They walked in silence as Jackson waited for Lucas to come to his senses and apologize but the boy remained stubbornly silent.

Shaking his head, Jackson finally said, "Until you

learn how to treat your mother with the respect she deserves, we won't be going riding again."

"That's not fair!"

Jackson glanced over at Lucas. "No, the way you've been treating your mother isn't fair. She's done nothing but love you unconditionally."

"She took my dad from me," he blurted out, tears filling his eyes.

"An *accident* took your father from you," Jackson corrected, his tone softening.

"You're wrong," the boy said. "She was mad at my dad and they got into a fight. She made him leave the party early. If she hadn't, he would still be alive."

Jackson stopped walking and turned to Lucas in surprise. "Where is this coming from? I know your mother wouldn't have told you something like that." Lainie had made it clear that she had done her best to spare her son the details of that fateful night. She'd done everything she could to protect him. To help him heal.

"She didn't tell me," Lucas confirmed. "I heard Lance's mom say it."

Jackson was troubled by that response. "Who is Lance?"

"My best friend back in Sacramento. We were out in the sunroom and his mom was in the kitchen talking to another lady who was at Lance's house visiting her. I heard them talking about my mom and dad. Mrs. Winters told the woman my mom and dad had words at his work party, and they left right after that. She said my dad would still be alive if my mom hadn't made him leave early." Tears ran in twin rivers down Lucas's cheeks, tearing at Jackson's heart.

Releasing the reins he'd been grasping so tightly in

frustration, Jackson pulled the sobbing boy into his comforting embrace. "Lucas." He sighed, finally understanding the depth of his anger and hurt. His heart went out to Lucas, for the emotional damage that false information had done, and to Lainie for the pain she, too, had suffered because of it.

"I hate her," he cried into Jackson's shirt, his horse's reins dangling from his clenched hand.

"Mrs. Winters was wrong," Jackson told him. "The accident wasn't your mother's fault. And shame on her for saying so, even if she didn't realize you were listening. Gossip is never something to be taken to heart. It can take the truth and twist it, hurting so many innocent people, like you and your mother."

Lucas lifted his tear-streaked face. "But it's not gossip. Mr. Winters w-worked with my dad," he said with a hiccupping sob. "They were at the party that night."

Tucker's advice to Lainie that day in the barn came to mind at that moment. *The truth can set you free.* "They may have been there, but only your mother knows what really happened that night. I can tell you that she loved your father very much and his dying broke her heart every bit as much as it did yours."

"But they had a fight."

"We don't know that," he said calmly. "Mrs. Winters might have misunderstood what was going on. And even if your parents did have a disagreement of some sort, that doesn't mean they didn't love each other deeply. Love isn't always a smooth road. Disagreements happen between people. But if they truly care for one another, they'll find a way to work things out."

"Did you love my mom?"

The question took Jackson off guard. "Did I?"

"Mrs. Winters said my dad was upset that night and told my mom she had never gotten over her first love," he stated knowingly, his sobs slowing to a few loud sniffles. "And then I heard Uncle Justin telling my mom she needed to work through whatever it was that had kept the two of you apart." He hesitated a moment before saying, "She told him that she had loved you when she was young and foolish. That your heart was already taken by the rodeo. Does that make you her first love?" he asked, a hint of accusation in his voice. Not that Jackson blamed him. The boy, slowly putting two and two together with what facts he thought he knew, probably harbored a bit of resentment toward Jackson now as well.

"You really need to stop listening in on conversations that don't involve you," Jackson chided.

"I didn't mean to," Lucas said in his own defense. "I went downstairs because a tree branch was scratching at my window and they were in the front room talking. Actually, my mom was crying. I didn't know what to do, so I stood there waiting."

Poor kid. Always seemed to be in the wrong place at the wrong time. Jackson released him and looked away, remembering. "Your mom and I were very close growing up," he answered honestly. "And she has always held a very special place in my heart. But the Lord sent us down different paths. Mine leading to the rodeo and the rodeo business my brothers and I have today. Your mom's led her to college, where she met your dad and fell in love. They married, giving her the biggest blessing in life—you."

"Have you and my mom worked things out?"

"Yes," Jackson replied with a nod. "We talked things

out and made things right again between us. The same as you two will." He looked down into misty, hazel-colored eyes. "But you need to tell her what you've told me. Give her a chance to answer your questions, even if what she has to say may be hard to hear. I care about you both deeply. There's nothing I want more than your happiness." He meant that from the bottom of his heart. Just as Lainie had done, Lucas had thoroughly embedded himself in Jackson's. He was the son Jackson had never had.

"I don't know if I can," Lucas said sadly.

"Do it for your dad then," Jackson suggested. "He loved your mom very much. I know he wouldn't want to see her hurting the way she is. Or you, for that matter. Talk to your mom and hear what she has to say. And then listen with your heart. It'll know the *real* truth when it hears it."

Lucas stood contemplating what Jackson had told him, the toe of his boot digging into the dirt at his feet.

"Lucas," Jackson prompted.

The boy looked up, agony in those young eyes. "I miss my dad."

"I know you do, son. But you're still blessed with a mother who loves you. I pray you'll give her a chance to tell you what really happened that night."

Lucas let out a heavy sigh and then nodded. "Okay, I'll do it."

Jackson sent up a silent prayer of thanks to the Lord. Lainie's son might be reluctant to talk to his mom, but he would soon learn the truth—and perhaps begin to heal.

Lainie stood up from the sofa at the sound of the front door opening. Her son's words had cut deep. Her own actions had cut even deeper. She had never run out on Lucas before, no matter how bad things got. But she had done so today, from the past, from the pain, from her son. Shame filled her.

"Lainie?" Jackson called out tentatively.

"In here," she called back, her stomach still in knots.

Jackson stepped into the garland-decorated entryway. "You walked home."

"I needed the walk," she told him. After putting Annie back in her stall in Jackson's barn, she'd practically run back to her brother's place. She'd known Jackson would see her son safely home when they were done riding.

"Lucas," Jackson said. A moment later, her son stepped around him.

Lainie's gaze zeroed in on her son's tear-streaked face. One that no doubt matched her own. And her heart broke. "Lucas," she said, moving to take him in her arms.

He took a step back, making it clear he didn't want her coddling.

"Lucas has some things he'd like to say to you," Jackson told her.

Looking down into her son's upturned face, she said, "I'm sorry I rode away like that." If her son was going to apologize, she should as well.

"Jackson said I should ask you for the truth," Lucas said instead and then followed it up with, "Were you fighting with my dad the night he got killed?"

Completely taken aback by her son's question, Lainie's desperate gaze shot up to meet Jackson's, finding concern there. Not even a flicker of surprise. How could he have pushed Lucas to ask things that would only be hurtful to him? He knew how she felt about protecting her son from any more pain.

"Was that why you and my dad left the party?" her son pressed when Lainie failed to respond to his question.

"I…" she said, faltering for a reply. "Lucas, honey, I need to see Jackson out. Then we can talk." And maybe by then she would have pulled herself back together enough to have this conversation she'd never wanted to have with her son.

Jackson looked to Lucas. "Remember what I told you, and try to listen with your heart," he told him before starting for the door. "It'll know the truth."

Lainie followed, both angry and hurt at Jackson's betrayal. The second she closed the porch door behind her, she swung around to confront Jackson. "How could you?" she demanded. "I thought you cared about my son. About me."

Regret filled his eyes. "I do. That's why I thought it best—" he began.

"Don't," she said, throwing up a hand to stop his explanation. There was no explanation that would make her understand his reasoning in pushing her son to demand the truth from her. "You have no right deciding what is best for my child. Opening him up to the pain my answering his questions is going to bring him is not even close to showing us you care. Maybe the Lord knew what he was doing in making him Will's son and not yours."

Her heart ached as she said the hurtful words, but something in Lainie had broken. There was nothing left in her to keep her calm. To keep the pain she felt at bay. And like her son, it seemed all she could do was hurt someone she cared so deeply about. "I think it would be best if you stayed away from my son," she said, barely able to see him through the blur of unshed tears that filled her eyes. "Away from me."

"Lainie, there's something you need to know."

She shook her head. "I can't do this, Jackson. Not right now. I have to see to my son."

He gave a slow nod. "Agreed. But know that I don't regret my actions. Not when it might help Lucas heal emotionally." Turning, he walked away, his limp more pronounced than normal. Probably from the ride he'd accompanied them on that afternoon. Despite the anger she felt toward Jackson at that moment, she also felt the loss of what they had worked so hard to rebuild—their friendship. And now that was gone as well.

With a muffled sob, Lainie stepped back into the house to face even more pain as she prepared herself to answer her son's questions about that fateful night. *Lord, help me to be strong for Lucas's sake. Give me the grace to face what is to come, and the ability to speak the words needed to heal Lucas's heart.*

"Are you mad at Mr. Wade?" her son asked when she returned to find him sitting anxiously on the sofa.

"What I am," she said as she moved to sit next to him on the sofa, "is worried about you." Then, praying for courage, she said, "Talk to me, Lucas. Ask me whatever it is you want to know."

And so he did, telling her everything he had told Jackson. Telling her what Jackson had told him. Or at least as much as a troubled eight-year-old boy could remember.

Lainie stood and walked over to stand before the lit Christmas tree, her heart wrenching as she stared up at the precious star Jackson had been so honored to place atop the tree she had chosen. He *hadn't* betrayed her. Guilt filled her. She had reacted emotionally, without all the facts, just as her son had with her. Jackson had only their best interests at heart, and she had accused him wrongly, immediately shutting him out of their lives. *Oh, Jackson.*

"Mom?"

She turned slowly, then told her son what had really happened that night. The truth was far better than Lucas living the rest of his life believing the more painful words of busybodies. That gossip that had torn what was left of her family apart and caused her to hurt the man she had never stopped loving all over again.

"Mr. Wade?"

The bale of hay Jackson had been about to toss froze in midair, its weight dragging his arms downward. Releasing it, he turned from where he stood in the bed of his truck to see Lucas standing next to the barn.

"Lucas," he said, jumping down to ground. The boy was a sight for sore eyes. He glanced around, expecting to see Lainie, whom he also hadn't seen for days. She'd called. He hadn't answered. She'd texted. He'd deleted his messages. It was for the best. He'd been a fool thinking there could be more between them. A future. The life he'd given away so many years ago. But her words about the Lord knowing what he was doing when he made Will Lucas's father had cut deep.

"Mom's not here," the boy said, as if reading Jackson's mind. "Uncle Justin brought me," he added, pointing off toward the SUV parked in the drive. "I told him I wanted to talk to you by myself."

"Does your mom know you're here?" he asked. Because Lainie had specifically told him to keep away from her son.

"No," he answered with a frown. "She's probably at home still."

That grabbed hold of Jackson's gut and twisted hard. "You shouldn't be here without your mom's knowing it," he told him. Even if he had missed spending time with Lucas, and Lainie, for that matter.

"I had to come," he told him. "I wanted to tell you I'm sorry."

"Sorry? For what?"

"For causing my mom to be upset with you," the boy admitted with a frown. "She was happy before I ruined everything."

"It's not your fault," Jackson told him, reaching out to tousle Lucas's hair. "She was upset, and sometimes when people are upset they unintentionally hurt those closest to them."

"Like I did to her," he acknowledged.

Jackson nodded. "Did you talk to your mom about what Mrs. Winters said?"

"Yeah, and you were right. Mrs. Winters was wrong," he told Jackson. "I know it now. My heart told me so."

Jackson's own heart lightened at the news. "So you and your mom are good?"

"I told her I won't ever be mean to her again and she forgave me."

"Of course she would," Jackson told him. "Your mother loves you."

"You, too," he said. Then reaching into the back pocket of his jeans, he withdrew his fisted hand. "I wanted to give this to you."

Holding out his upturned hand, Jackson watched as Lucas opened his and turned it as if placing something precious into the awaiting palm. But when he pulled away, there was nothing there. Jackson looked to him questioningly.

"It's my birthday wish," Lainie's son explained. "The one I stuck in my pocket to use later. That's why I asked Uncle Justin to bring me here. To give it to you. I thought maybe you could use it to make things right with my mom again. She misses you. I miss you."

Curling his hand as if to protect the gift he'd just been given, Jackson felt the burn of tears at the backs of his eyes. "I miss you, too." And how he longed to have them back in his life again. Holding up his clenched hand, he said, "I won't let this go to waste." Then he made as if to store it in the pocket of his jacket for safekeeping.

Surprising him once more, Lucas stepped forward, wrapping his arms around Lucas's waist. "I love you, Mr. Wade." Then he broke away and ran off.

Jackson watched him go, his heart filled with emotion. Lucas climbed into the car with his uncle and then with a wave from his best friend, they pulled away. "I love you, too, Lucas," he said, emotion filling his voice. Just as he loved Lainie. With all his heart.

"And here I thought I had the art of avoidance down to a T."

For the second time that day, an unexpected visitor took Jackson by surprise. Only this time, he was beyond shocked. Lowering the fly rod he'd been about to cast out, he set it down along the edge of the slow-flowing river and turned to face her. He'd gone there to mull over everything Lucas had told him and decide on a plan of action. But the woman in his thoughts had just stepped out of them and in front of him, causing his heart to slam against his chest.

Lainie stood about twenty feet away, at the edge of the woods. Her face looked pale, strained. Yet she was still the most beautiful woman he'd ever known. As if in agreement, his heartbeat kicked into overdrive.

"I saw your truck parked by the road. Your mother told me you had gone into town," she said, anxiety lacing her voice.

"I intended to," he replied. "Changed my mind. Figured I'd come out here to fish instead."

"In the cold?" she said as she started toward him down the gently sloping bank.

Cold seemed to be a good means to numb the pain of missing Lainie but being unsure how to put things back to the way they'd been. He'd prayed about it long and hard. He'd talked to his brothers in the days since his and Lainie's fallout. Even Justin had done his best to convince Jackson to call his sister and work things out. He'd even gone so far as to make use of Lucas's gift—the birthday wish he'd given him—and then chided himself for wasting his time on something so silly. But after Lucas's visit, Jackson knew there was something worth fighting for.

"Fish still bite when it's cold," he told her. He glanced around. "Where's Lucas?"

"He's spending the day with Justin," she replied. "I think they were going to visit Jessica."

"So you walked over in this cold?" he noted.

"Actually, I drove."

"Excuse me?"

"I had my brother drive me into town yesterday to pick up my new truck. Figured I would need it to hunt you down, since you've been avoiding my calls."

"You drove here by yourself?" he said, amazed at what she'd pushed herself to do on account of him.

"I would have driven to the ends of the earth if it meant finding you, so I could do what I've been trying to do for days." Her expression grew serious. "Jackson, I'm so sorry for the way I reacted when you brought Lucas home to talk to me. I never should have said the things I did to you."

"You thought I'd broken your trust," he acknowledged, seeing the pain of regret in her eyes.

"If I had been thinking clearly," she began and then shook her head. "No, that's no excuse. I was wrong, and I can't bear knowing that I hurt you. Truth is I regretted my actions the moment the words left my mouth." She looked up at him. "Please tell me I haven't lost you for good."

He found himself reaching out to caress her cheek. "Never."

"Jackson," she said in a low voice.

He smiled down at her. "You are far too important to me to let a moment decide my forever. And I hope you know that I would never have gone against your wishes, but when Lucas told me what that woman had said, his behavior toward you finally made sense. You were the only person who could respond to the gossip and the ridiculous claim that you and Will had been fighting that night over me."

Lainie glanced away, falling silent.

"Lainie?"

"It's true," she said with a soft sob. "Will wasn't a

drinker, but during that night several of his coworkers brought him over to toast his success with them. The excess of liquor became too much for my husband to handle. I pulled him aside at the party and told him we needed to leave before he said, or did, something he might regret. His response was, 'The way you regret not marrying your first love.'" She looked away. "His words hurt, because I had been honest with him about my feelings for you and he'd said that he understood. I'd made it clear to him right from the beginning that I had married him because I loved him and wanted the life we had together. But he wasn't in the right mental frame of mind that night to have that discussion, so I insisted we leave." She closed her eyes, tears rolling down her cheeks.

Jackson drew her into his arms, smoothing a comforting hand up and down her back. "Will wasn't himself," he said tenderly. "He didn't mean the things he said."

"I think he did," she said sadly. "He knew I couldn't give my whole heart to him. Not when a part of it belonged to you, would always belong to you. I was so upset with him that night, and filled with guilt, as I drove him home, I couldn't even bear to look at my husband, which is why I never saw the other car running through the red light."

"Oh, Lainie Girl," he groaned, wrapping his arms tighter around her. He wanted more than anything to make the hurt go away. But that was something she needed to work through herself. All he could do was be there for her.

She lifted her face from his now-tear-dampened jacket front. "Why do I always hurt the men that I love?

Will died because of me," she said, her voice catching. "And *you* nearly died because of me."

He shook his head. "Lainie, no."

"Yes," she reiterated. "You were on your way to winning that rodeo championship until I called. I should've realized the date, known where you would be. But all I could think about was calling you with the news of my engagement. A part of me wanted you to regret what you had given up, even though I had already moved on with my life."

"I hurt you first," he said quietly.

"I called you about my engagement before I even told my family," she admitted. "I shouldn't have cared about your reaction. Shouldn't have called you at all. I know that. I've carried the guilt of that day with me for years. Will deserved better from me. *You* deserved better from me. And I know in my heart that my call had something to do with your getting thrown that day. You were too good. If you had died that day..." Her words trailed off.

"I didn't die," he said, pressing a tender kiss to her brow. "But I finally understood what they mean when they say regret is a hard pill to swallow. I had never regretted anything as much in my life as that moment I let you go."

Her head lifted, her eyes searching his. "You were better off letting me go. You see what happens to the men I give my heart to."

"I never once blamed you for what happened to me that day. The fault was mine." He should never have taken that ride if his head wasn't in the game.

"Jackson," she said, emotion clear in her tone, "if anything had happened to you..."

"It didn't. And you seem to forget that I'm a cowboy. We're a tough breed," he told her with a tender smile. "I'll always be here for you, Lainie. Always." That said, he lowered his head and kissed her tenderly.

Chapter Ten

"Is that cinnamon bread I smell?" Justin asked when he stepped into the kitchen, his hair still mussed from sleep.

She turned from the stove, a pecan-topped pan held in her oven-mitt-covered hands. "Fresh from the oven," she said.

He looked to her, blinking. "Is that a smile I see on your face?"

"It might be."

A grin tugged at his lips as he moved farther into the room. "Anything to do with Jackson?"

Lainie felt ready to burst with happiness, having finally set things right with Jackson the day before. Jackson loved her, always had. "Yes."

He nodded. "Glad to hear it. Lucas has been fretting himself sick over your being a walking, talking waterworks display before now, and Jackson's being absent from your lives."

Her brother had comforted her after she'd ordered Jackson from her life and had then realized, too late, how badly she had misunderstood the situation. He'd even offered to talk to Jackson, who was ignoring Lainie's texts and calls, but she'd asked him to let her mend her own broken fences. Which, thank the Lord, she'd been able to do. For her sake as well as her son's. She thought back to the kiss she and Jackson had shared. One that had ended so differently from their first. It had been a declaration of the love they felt for each other, and a promise of the direction they wanted their relationship to move in.

"I feel like my prayers have finally been answered," she told her brother as she turned to set the hot pan on top of the stove. "I truly believe the Lord brought Jackson back into my life to help me get my sweet little boy back." Ever since she had answered Lucas's questions, gently but honestly, he had become the son she had feared forever lost to her. Thankfully, the questions he'd had for her that day were simple and to the point. She hadn't needed to go into detail about everything, like the extent of Will's injuries. They had, however, discussed how alcohol had impaired Will's ability to think rationally. That while Jackson had been her first love, Lucas's father was the man she had pledged her love to in the eyes of God, and she missed him so very much.

"I'd like to think I might have played a small part in that as well," Justin teased with a grin.

"You did, and I will be forever grateful for your having guilted him into riding back into my life." She thought back to that first day arriving home and how her heart had reacted when she'd seen Jackson seated atop his horse. As if she recognized a part of it beat within that man.

He chuckled. "Whatever it took to see the two of you rebuilding your broken friendship."

Pulling off the oven mitts, she tossed them onto the counter and then stepped forward to place a kiss on her brother's cheek. "I love you, big brother."

"I love you, too, baby sister," he replied, his smile holding such warmth.

"Mom!" Lucas called out from the front room, where he'd been watching a movie. "Mr. Wade's here!"

Lainie's heart skipped a beat. Jackson was there? He was supposed to be helping Garrett with the herd's blood withdrawals for the biannual health record updates.

"Can't stay away from you, I see," her brother said with a teasing grin.

She knew the feeling. Lainie hurried from the room, but Lucas had already beaten her to the door and was out on the porch waving to Jackson, who was striding toward them.

He gave a wave back, a grin spreading across his face.

Her son did what Lainie longed to do—he ran and threw himself into Jackson's strong arms.

Jackson's husky chuckle rent the air as he swung her son around. He set Lucas back onto his feet, gave his hair a fond ruffle and then fixed his gaze on Lainie.

"Lainie Girl," he greeted with such tenderness she thought she might burst into tears of happiness.

"What are you doing here?" she asked, unable to keep the smile from her face. "I thought you were supposed to be helping Garrett this morning." At least, that's what he'd said when they'd had their talk the day before.

"Tucker had a little extra time on his hands, so he offered to relieve me of my duty, so I could ride over and see you and Lucas. Actually, he insisted. He says I'll be as useless as feathers on a fish until I've gotten to look in on you two. Truth is, I missed spending time with the two of you."

"We missed you, too!" Lucas said excitedly.

"I can vouch for that," Justin agreed with a grin.

They were right, Lainie thought as she took in the handsome cowboy in front of her, with his boyish grin and broad shoulders. Shoulders that had helped her bear the weight of her burdens so many times since coming home. She hadn't realized just how much she had looked forward to seeing Jackson with each new day until he'd stopped coming—at her request. And now that they had made up, her world felt right again.

"I'm glad you stopped by," she said, meaning it from the very bottom of her heart.

His grin widened, drawing her gaze to his mouth. Her thoughts went back to the kiss they'd shared, a silent declaration of their hearts. Then her gaze lifted to meet his, and she felt his love wrap around her.

"Will you take us riding today?" Lucas asked, drawing their attention. "I've been really nice to my mom. Haven't I, Mom?" he asked, looking up at her.

She nodded, her son having told her what Jackson had said about his not riding until he learned to treat her better. "My sweet, loving boy is back."

"Glad to hear it," he replied, and then turned his gaze to Lucas. "I've got time for us to take a short ride before I have to go back to the ranch to help Garrett and Tucker. But you need to see if it's all right with your mom first. She might have other plans."

They looked to Lainie.

She shook her head. "No plans whatsoever."

"Yay!" her son exclaimed, pumping his little fist into the air.

"Would you two mind if I had a few words with Lainie in private first?" Jackson asked, his attention fixed on Lainie.

"Come on, kiddo," Justin said with a nod. "Let's give your mom and Jackson some breathing room."

Lucas followed her brother into the house, closing the door behind them.

Lainie looked up at Jackson. "He's really happy to see you."

His grin displayed that adorable Wade dimple. "I'm hoping he's not the only one."

"No," she said softly, "he's not. Not only am I glad to see you, I'm so thankful you chose to forgive me."

"I'm sorry you had to hunt me down for that forgiveness," he said. "I should have given it to you sooner instead of avoiding your calls."

"I can't blame you for not wanting to talk to me," she admitted. "What I said—about the Lord knowing what He was doing in making him Will's son and not yours—was spoken out of hurt and anger, as well as guilt. You would make a wonderful father to any child. Don't ever think otherwise. I'm ashamed to have even spoken those words."

"Why the guilt?" he asked.

Lainie hadn't even realized she'd said that word until he questioned her about it. With a frown, she said, "Because there were times when I'd look at my son and I found myself wondering what my life might have been like had you and I ended up together and Lucas had been your son. And then I would tell myself to let the past go. Let you go. Focus on all that I had been blessed with, because I had been blessed. But you were always there in my thoughts."

"You were always there in mine, too," he admitted.

"You might not be the father of my son," she said, "but you are the one who gave him back to me when I thought I had lost my son for good. Christmas truly is a season of blessings."

"I'm glad to have helped," he answered humbly. "And, speaking of Christmas, I was wondering if you and Lucas might like to accompany me to the holiday social and dance on Christmas Eve?"

The holiday gathering was to be held following Christmas Eve church services. Everyone she knew would be there, including her parents, who hadn't missed the town's holiday social since adopting Lainie and her brother. Her thoughts drifted back to the last dance she'd gone to and how it had ended so badly. If only she had known then what she knew now. That Jackson had loved her enough to let her go.

Lainie's hesitation had Jackson's confidence slipping several notches. What had he been thinking, asking her to a dance of all things? He was no longer that same fearless, rodeo-riding youth she'd once shared a dance with. "Forget I asked," he said, embarrassment heating the skin beneath his shirt collar. "I should have considered my bum leg before extending my invitation. There will be far better dance partners willing to take you out onto the dance floor."

"I don't want another dance partner," she told him with a tender smile. "I want you, Jackson Wade, bum leg and all. Because I adore you. And that tiny little hitch you have in your step doesn't make you any less of a catch for any woman. It only tells me you're a man with not only outer strength, but inner as well. You're not a quitter. When the doctors feared you might never walk again, you set your mind to prove them wrong. You've held on to your faith when others might not have. You're kind and compassionate. And don't get me started on that dimple of yours."

Emotion knotted in his throat. "You like my dimple?" he said playfully, when all he could think about was how much he loved this woman.

Lainie rolled her eyes. "Oh please. Show me a woman who doesn't get weak-kneed over a handsome cowboy with a boyish dimple. You are the perfect catch for any woman, and don't you ever doubt that."

"A man could get used to your kind of flattery," he said, his gaze drawn to movement in the living room window that faced the porch. "I think someone's anxious to go on that ride." He gave a nod, motioning toward the smiling face peering back at them from the other side of the windowpane.

Lainie laughed. "Appears so. We'll change into something warmer for the ride and then drive over to your place."

"I don't mind waiting if you want to ride over with me."

"No," she told him. "This is something I need to do. For me."

"Proud of you." He clearly wasn't the only one with inner strength. Lainie had a good bit of grit in her, too. His Lainie Girl, who had never stopped loving him.

Now it was his turn to put his heart on his sleeve and take that chance he pushed away all those years ago.

Lainie felt like a teenage girl again, her heart all aflutter, as Jackson accompanied her and Lucas to the Christmas social. Even though they had already spent the entire morning and part of the afternoon together, this felt different. Maybe it was because she remembered all too well how the last dance she'd shared with Jackson had ended. She just prayed she would be able to keep her feelings for Jackson to herself this time. She cared too much to risk losing what they had, even if she longed for so much more.

"Lainie," Autumn said as she came over to give her an affectionate hug. "Thank you so much for helping with the basket drive."

She smiled. "Thank you so much for including me. It felt so good to be a part of something so special."

"The reverend was so pleased with how it turned out he's already planning for next year's charity drive."

"Sign me up," Lainie offered excitedly.

"I'll let him know," Autumn said as her gaze shifted. "Looks like Blue found the cookie table. I'd better go make sure she leaves a few for everyone else."

Laughing softly, Lainie watched her friend walk away. Her thoughts drifted back to earlier that morning when she and Jackson had gone out together to deliver the baskets they'd been assigned. The surprise and then the emotion that had come over the recipients' faces was something she would never forget. And the feeling it had given her in her heart was beyond describable. She vowed to be a part of the charity basket collection every year and intended to seek out other opportunities to make a difference in others' lives.

Turning back to face the milling crowd, she caught sight of her parents, who stood talking to the Dawsons across the room. The four old friends were all smiles, clearly enjoying that evening's festivities. It was good to see her parents out and about, enjoying themselves. And her father looked to be holding up surprisingly well, considering the long day he was putting in. After they had finished delivering the baskets, Jackson had come over to her brother's place for her family's annual Christmas Eve lunch. Jessica and her son had come as well, at her brother's invitation.

Lainie had to admit he had never seemed happier. More surprisingly, Justin had invited them to spend Christmas Day with him. The man who would have rather worked than sit around admiring a lit Christmas tree. A true Christmas miracle. Lucas had even asked Jackson to help him string more popcorn for the tree, because, according to her son, there wasn't near enough on there. It had warmed her heart, watching the two of them together, creating new Christmas memories. Happy ones. And now she was here, in the church's festively decorated social hall, surrounded by family and friends, celebrating the great blessing the Lord had bestowed upon them when He sent His Son into the world to be born.

"I believe this is our dance."

She turned to find Jackson standing there, a wide smile gracing his handsome face. "You're claiming the first one?" she said teasingly.

"I'm claiming all of them," he told her as he led her out onto the floor.

She glanced around, expecting other dancers to follow. Instead, everyone, including both of their families, formed a wide circle around them. "What are they doing?" she whispered anxiously to Jackson as all eyes turned their way.

"Giving me the opportunity to do this," he said as he turned to face her, dropping down onto one knee.

Lainie gasped, her hand coming to rest on her suddenly pounding heart. "Jackson," she breathed. This was the moment she had dreamed of for so long, but suddenly felt so unprepared for. Her legs trembled beneath her as she stood looking down at him, searching his handsome face. Oh, how she loved this man.

"Lainie Girl," he began, his eyes glinting with an even deeper tenderness than she'd ever recalled seeing in them, "Christmas is filled with blessings and you are mine. I've loved you for what feels like an eternity, but I had to be patient and allow the Lord to bring you back to me. And now here you are with your beautiful smile and tender, always-giving heart." He withdrew a small box from the front pocket of his dress pants and opened the lid. "I love not only you, but your son as well. And while I would never seek to replace his father, I'd be honored to be the man he looks up to for guidance when he needs advice. Lainie Dawson Michaels, will you make me the happiest cowboy in all of Wyoming this Christmas and agree to become my wife?"

Everything seemed so surreal. So much so, Lainie found herself praying she wasn't dreaming this moment. Her gaze came to rest on the pear-shaped diamond sparkling beneath the tiny white lights strung over the dance floor. Then she looked up into Jackson's loving eyes and knew this was the moment she had waited a lifetime for. She also knew in her heart that Will would have wanted her and Lucas to move on with their lives. To find happiness again. To become a real family.

"Just so you know," Jackson added with a lone-dimpled grin as he waited for her answer, "I've already asked your father, your brother and your son for their blessings."

"We said yes!" Lucas hollered from somewhere in the crowd.

Laughing happily, Lainie nodded, tears filling her eyes. Her son's approval meant the world to her. Now they could be a family, building a new life together in the only place she ever really thought of as home, surrounded by those they loved. "Yes, Jackson," she said, her heart overflowing with happiness, "I'll marry you. And I promise to spend every day of my life loving you just as deeply as I do today."

Easing the ring from its velvety bed, he held it up to Lainie. "I'd like for you to read the inscription on the inside of the band before I place it on your finger."

Taking the precious offering, she brought it closer, tilting it ever so slightly as she read the words he'd had inscribed inside, her heart melting: YOU ARE MY WISH.

"Lucas was kind enough to give me his unused birthday wish," he explained. "And your love is what I wished for. Prayed for. Yearned for."

"It's beautiful," she told him, beyond touched by his incredibly thoughtful gesture. "Both on the inside and out. And just so *you* know," she said, repeating his earlier words, "you've always had my love."

Sliding the ring onto her finger, Jackson stood and then drew her into his arms for a tender kiss that promised her a lifetime of tomorrows.

* * * * *

Dear Reader,

I really hope you've had a chance to read the first two books in my Bent Creek Blessings series—*The Cowboy's Little Girl* and *The Rancher's Baby Surprise*. *Hometown Christmas Gift* is the third and final book in this Love Inspired series, giving the last of the Wade brothers, Jackson, his very own happily-ever-after. It's a story of healing and second chances for both my hero, Jackson, and Lainie, his first love. It's about turning to one's faith to help carry us through the hard times and knowing that God has a plan for us all. It's also discovering that not all Christmas gifts are ones you can hold in your hand, like the gift of forgiveness, the gift of hope and the gift of happiness. Things that both Lainie and Jackson gift each other with in *Hometown Christmas Gift*. I hope you enjoy reading their story as much as I enjoyed writing it. For updates on my upcoming releases, you can go to my website at www.lindseybrookes.com or follow Kat Brookes on Facebook. The link to my homepage is https://www.facebook.com/kat.brookes.5.

Happy holidays!
Kat